"Harrowing Roses is a story of intoxicating romance.
There is some sort of intuition, a tantalizing connection between the two romantic leads, and Cooper does an excellent job of keeping us on our toes. Their mistrust of each other is exciting, dangerous, and it is all wrapped into a desire for one another that neither can deny."

– Madeline Barbush, Independent Book Review

"What a perfectly chilling story!
Cooper's style of writing really sets the perfect mood."

– Deborah Dove, author

ISBN: 978-1-7397172-8-5

HARROWING ROSES

BARBARA COOPER

Prologue

IT WAS SOMETHING INCREDIBLE. Her vivacious energy in bed. With her, he had felt such pleasure and distress at the same time.

It was like there was something inside of her that needed to be filled.

She was on top of him. She let out short breaths, as though they were her last...gasping for air.

She did it all with such intensity – and he sensed an emotion akin to distress.

It was if a ravine opened inside of her.

Her body, always so pale, was turning redder, almost dark purple...in the dim lights of his cabin...on his spacious bed.

Then, after that moment, she got up and he observed her nude, tanned skin, as she carried herself to the bathroom – unashamed and seductively curving, like a silver-screen goddess.

Jonathan guessed that in a few moments' time, she would leave, and he wouldn't see her no more, and indeed she left the cabin a short while later.

But he would be seeing Dana again, sometime soon.

The wind was howling. Henry had closed the window tightly, so the cold would not be getting inside.

The outside temperature had dropped significantly. The darkness around was pitch black, only interrupted in a few places by a light-grey fog settling on the surface of the lakes...the wetlands, to be precise.

He had dreamed again. He had dreamed about her, again. He tossed and turned on his small wooden bed. There wasn't much furniture around him, just the basic necessities of a small cabin.

He dreamed about the future, the past and the present. He detected a buzz of sounds, actions, unknown to him, unfamiliar. All foggy, elusive, untouchable – difficult to remember, difficult to place.

About fog coming from the lake and dark sounds, covering all of it.

But underneath the changes, one thing stayed the same – a constant whisper, talking to him without end.

It was her – Dana. A slight breeze moved through her fiery, strawberry-copper hair.

He knew it was important. That she was important. Not why though, at least not now.

But he barely knew her.

He didn't even like her that much.

Dana's blue eyes were light, but dark in their nature…and in the background, just the murky greyness of dark clouds and deep waters. Then her eyes, looking straight ahead, were turning dark grey as the stormy sky.

But this won't even matter after all, that much he knew – this, that is yet to happen.

This is a story of murder. Of course it didn't start like that, but all is not black and white. The trajectory of things can go in unforeseen and unexpected directions.

So please be kind.

Chapter I

DANA WAS SITTING BY THE TABLE, LOOKING AT HER MOTHER NEARBY, POURING THE TEA INTO THE CUPS THAT THE MAID HAD BROUGHT IN.

Her youngish mother was like a porcelain doll – her best pearls at her neck, beautifully maintained long blonde hair reaching onto her back, which was now falling into her eyes delicately as she was putting in the sugar.

Dana could hear the clock slowly ticking on the mantel. She looked around the room. They were together in the afternoon drawing room. She was her mother's daughter in every way, now 22 years old, with a slim tallish figure, nicely curved – to all appearances, already a woman. Her thick naturally reddish hair ended a little below her shoulders. Her every move, if you looked closely enough, held a promise of granting every wish you might ever have. Her face was a blooming beauty in the making, just of the right age to be able to make something of it...to be something...to ask people for whatever she wanted, or thought she wanted. Her blue eyes were flecked with green, which she got from her father.

Dana was now sitting by the dining table, looking out of the window. It was unusually bright outside for this winter season; sunlight danced on the light cloth of the luxurious orange-silvery curtains that framed the big round windows. Mother had sent the maid away.

Lately, they had preferred to be alone, together, in private.

They kept to themselves.

They were here for reasons that are much too complicated to explain, but this is where they would stay for a while. She was with her mother...just them now.

'Here' was the country estate belonging to her father's side of the family, near the open wetlands, just on the edge of civilisation. This was where her father grew up.

Her father's family had always liked it out here – they'd never thought of a reason to relocate anywhere else. But her father had! He spread his wings far away from here for sure. Thanks to this, Dana was a city girl right from the beginning, when she was a very young child, and she hadn't come to visit family very much when growing up.

So, naturally, their money had always come from a different source, further away from these barren wastelands.

But this visit was very important for her and her mother. And for their future.

And here they would prevail or, if that failed, they would go and find a different situation elsewhere if they didn't fit in, weren't wanted here – now that her father was gone.

Today they sat alone, away from the rest of the family. They were trying to shelter themselves from the tension; it was palpable.

But who were they trying to fool? It had always been like this as long as she could remember.

Now, as they were sitting here quietly together, she reflected that it had only been two days since her cousin – Debra Lee, daughter of her uncle – had gone missing.

There was no news. Nothing from the police.

Dana didn't even miss her that much.

Chapter II

Henry was lying in bed; the night was drawing in...the moon was coming up and shining through the curtainless window.

The clock was ticking lazily, but as if every tick was filled with hidden meaning.

It had been two days tonight since the girl had gone missing.

It seemed as if the time around him suddenly started going more slowly now.

And he didn't know her at all, just of her.

The girl from the neighbouring house. Or should he say their mansion? So very different from his own dwelling.

They were only faraway neighbours...but still.

Chapter III

The next morning, she was restless – drawn to go outside, to look for the dark.

To go to the wetland, like always.

To see her lover.

Dana walked alone through the great expanse of uninviting nature. She enjoyed the hike. She was dressed in sports clothes; practical clothes that were warm and full of natural colour – bark-brown high boots, green and grey vest. So unlike the way she had dressed when at home.

It was sensible, because the ground was almost always wet.

Soaked vegetation leapt toward her and sometimes onto her – as if it wanted a piece of her for itself.

Around her was the start of the wetlands, a natural formation full of flowing and static water, which sooner or later found its way to the sea.

The vegetation was very rich around here, from high grasses and bushes to small trees, next to them were ponds which connected to larger waterways. This was more of an enclave in the deep forest that surrounded them.

A forest which had been shaped, thanks to the river, ages ago.

These parts were still easily accessible by foot, because there were wooden paths built into them, by human hand. Some of them went on firm land, some even above the water in places.

But to decide to stray off the path wasn't a good idea, at least not in this part of it, because you might venture into a territory of uneven and muddy swamps that aren't even easily visible. In the woods, the ground was higher and firm again.

She loved walking here, because it usually meant she was alone.

The weather was cold around here almost all the time, and cloudy.

She was getting closer to where the two cabins stood. By the lakes, a good distance from where the roads ended and the wetlands begin. Nothing was much civilised here, just the lonely cabins, accessible only by this wooden path through the waters and grass. Her destination was the second cabin, the further one.

She had reached the watery ponds already. Today their unmoving surface reflected the almost-black skies.

She meandered around them, the path getting thinner at places and difficult to navigate.

Why would anyone live here? That was a question. But she liked it here. That's why she came here, as often as she could. And also, because she couldn't wait to see her lover...

She came here just to be alone. Or, on the other hand, to have company, when she felt like it during her stay here at the mansion. A different kind of company indeed. She was sure her stay at her relatives' was short term, so why not have some fun while she was here, too? But what a time she and her mother had picked to visit.

"For a few weeks" she had said. *And then everything will be back in order, normal.* She would take care of it, she said. Then they would go home and carry on with their lives.

But now this had to happen!

The girl disappearing like that.

Putting an indefinite halt to all of their plans.

The family was terrified.

It had been two days since Debra Lee had gone missing, and she had not been heard of since.

As if time had started going by more slowly.

Debra Lee was her cousin.

A foolish young thing. She was now 17 years old, making Dana her elder.

Otherwise, she was difficult to describe. Dana didn't like Debra Lee. She just didn't care for her that much...

Dana considered herself to be very different. The others of the family actually thought that of her too – which was to be honest not always to Dana's advantage. She was not very close to her relatives, her father's brother and his family, and not even to her grandparents – even before all this happened.

And the visible dislike between the two cousins, her and Debra Lee, didn't help Dana's cause that much. Her cause being, of course, to be liked and accepted by her family. So only Mother was here – to make her feel protected and safe right now. That was good now that her father had gone away.

Anyhow, she felt like she was visiting a foreign family, not her own. The house was huge and beautiful, but nobody in it knew anything much about her or even cared about finding out. Her grandparents were very private people. They had opposed the marriage of her mother, Sheryl, to her father, their oldest son, right from the very beginning, many years ago. And the couple's only daughter's odd, uncontrolled and intangible nature wasn't getting her much nearer to winning their hearts, not even when she was just a small baby – brought here to close the divisions within the family once again. And then when she grew older, her father still didn't do that much to keep a close connection with family who were out here, 'living in the wilderness', much to his own dislike, so they never grew close again. Really, the whole mess of a situation was down to him!

As a young adult, whenever Dana and her mother had come here, to this house, they had been welcomed, given their own bedrooms and dining rooms in their own part of the house and so on, but otherwise they continued to live as if in a stranger's house.

Now, when they are in trouble, financial mostly, since their father has abandoned them, and will probably be needing the family – they are here.

"Just in case," her mother said, "we must try to get on their good side. You are so beautiful, so why not? If your father, isn't coming back anytime soon, we must try…"

They were originally just smalltown folks, after all, but with all that money…When Father had moved to the city, he started to take care of his own business, and he was happy there. Leaving his parents and his (at that time unmarried) brother behind.

Father never knew very much about his younger brother's new family; Mother always said he envied Father…having been able to get away to the big-city life, having the courage.

And having married the local oh-so-sought-after beauty queen, her, a short time before leaving them. He decided to marry Mother – as if she was something he could own. "Not a girl like that in sight around there!" this is what her father used to say to Dana, about her.

The atmosphere in the house didn't make Dana feel particularly welcome.

Her father's siblings, her aunts and uncles, never got that close or dear to her; they were divided by the places where they lived and the way in which they lived in the city, which was bound to lead to this, after all.

She agreed with her father on this – and wondered what kind of strange people would live all these years out here in the wilderness, in the wetland, with only a small town nearby, and its typical small-time vibes and flow? No good high-end shops nearby, no talk about schools with any prestige to attend. Her cousin Debra Lee had lived like this her whole life, without any other thought.

Don't get her wrong – Dana loved the wetlands, loved going outside, venturing, always looking for something new. But temporarily!

Otherwise she would feel the atmosphere of the marsh getting to her and slowly creeping under her skin...which was already happening in a way. Before long, it would start driving her crazy. So many open spaces, yet nowhere to go.

So many great hiding places, but with nothing interesting enough to hide.

But Debra Lee was nothing like that; she would never come out here. She liked to stay with both feet firmly on dry land, so to speak. To come here, wander aimlessly, just like Dana, even just for simple walk, was beneath her. How very highbrow of her.

It was a very smalltown attitude, Dana saw that. She had no problem telling Debra Lee that to her face. But not when the other relatives were around! In every sense of the word, Debra Lee was perfect in their eyes – commonly pretty, commonly smart... obedient. "If only her cousin Dana could be like her!" she could almost hear them say. Behind her back of course.

How ludicrous; comparing herself, her glorious self, to a smalltown younger girl!

So in that light, she didn't miss her at all. But still her unexpected, sudden and unexplained disappearance weighed on her family considerably.

She wanted to get out of the house.

But who was she kidding? She would have gone out to the wetland anyhow.

Lost in her thoughts about family ties, she was now almost reaching her destination.

Suddenly she came upon a small body of water, where there were wild flowers growing, almost in the water, but also all around it – wild flowers blooming.

She had stopped to admire the beauty of the dark red blooms. Were they waterlilies? They looked much too heavy for that.

So unnatural for them to be here, and at this time of year.

Never had she seen flowers like that before.

Having a closer look at the flowers now, she saw that they were like roses indeed.

While she admired the beauty of the flowers, they gave her a feeling of unexpected dread that sprung to the surface from the odd sensation of finding them here and now, as if they were an omen about her cousin, and her cousin's fate, reaching out to her.

Were the wetlands surrounding their mansion finally ready to keep a secret of their own? Were they ready to take Debra Lee from them…and swallow her whole?

What an irony, regarding her cousin's dislike of the wetlands, Dana thought.

They would be able to hide her in plain sight, never to be seen.

She turned around, felt as though someone was walking behind her. Towards her, she felt a shift in the air. But as she laid eyes on the back of the path, there was nothing there. No one.

She hurried further on, shivered a bit. But otherwise it was an exciting thought. She felt energised.

And now she was going to see Jonathan.

She passed the first cabin on the left.

Though she didn't stop, nor look around, still the thought of the present occupant and owner – a stranger, a person by the name of Henry – crept into her mind.

She didn't know him that well. Hardly at all.

He was quite a young guy, good looking and came from the city, just like her.

He came here on the weekends and so, alone.

He also wasn't a friend of Jonathan's, not particularly.

On the other hand, Jonathan stayed by the cabin by the lake full time, the whole week. It was like that at this point in his life, there was nowhere he was expected, or even wanted. Not now, anyhow.

His cabin had always been in his family. So, he decided to use it for himself.

She liked to take advantage of that fact; Jonathan and his cabin was the one constant for her – he took her boredom away. For a while anyhow…

He was living in the cabin at least for now, and Dana chose him to be her lover for the time she was here, at her family's home. A limited time, she was sure of that.

But she was fond of Jonathan, in a way. He had this unspoiled sweetness surrounding him, slowly going on thirty. In spite of his difficulties – things that he had had to go through lately, back in the town – he still remained like that – carefree. He was used to getting by only with his pretty face and so on. Now he was living here in the marshes, out of necessity, isolated – such a strange thing to do for such a young guy.

She kept him company while she could.

And contrary to what you might expect, despite living here, he was quite jovial, a good-spirited fellow.

Nothing too complicated about him.

Yet his neighbour, Henry, was different. There was something very mysterious about him.

Possibly in the past, she heard, he had been a soldier, or some such, from the military base, she didn't know. He came here, from time to time, to get away from it all, to be alone by the look of it. He kept to himself, got away from people.

When they were passing from time to time, he said hello to her – as he was supposed to, out of politeness. Now she smiled to herself. He seemed interesting enough to her.

But she in turn had definitely gotten the neighbour's interest.

Dana just didn't know about that, not now.

The morning was not over yet.

Chapter IV

SOMETIMES HENRY WISHED IT WAS ALL OVER. The slow bending of time: the monotonous days. All leading, usually, to nothing...the only certainty was the same bad weather.

But that day it was a little different.

Later around noon, she came and talked to him.

And what an unexpectedly strange experience the rest of the afternoon turned out to be for him.

Before that, he'd had a sense of anticipation of something happening; he could feel it in his bones, and the same the whole day before that – in his dreams, and this morning. He just believed his premonitions were possibly connected to her: the missing girl, Debra Lee, from the nearby house – not altogether connected with her cousin, Dana. Her presence here was not so unusual; she used to come a lot.

To back up a bit – it had been around 12 o'clock, and she, his red-headed faraway neighbour, had been visiting Jonathan next door.

He had been watching through his window – just casually, being slightly curious. And knowing that he could catch a glimpse of them from his kitchen window, from time to time, while they were inside the other cabin, moving around.

Otherwise he kept to himself and his own business, of course; he was not one for spying on his neighbours. He smiled at that thought, sitting by his work desk.

He was curious, with the disappearance of the girl and all, wondering what state the cousin would be in, or at least how would it manifest during her meeting with Jonathan.

She was unusually cheerful, or so it seemed – jumping around Jonathan, now outside his front door...as if excited.

Henry wasn't surprised, as he maybe should have been. He felt it too.

The slowly pulsing vibrations.

All around them.

Or so he imagined.

It looked as though she felt it too. As if something was happening.

Were they all part of an actual murder happening around them in real-time?

He turned off the stove. He lost his appetite for tea suddenly. It started to get stuffy inside.

He kept on watching…watching Jonathan's hand movements and gestures, his next-door neighbour wasn't as understanding as Henry.

Actually, Jonathan seemed horrified, even worried, about the way his lady visitor was acting. Henry was imagining the story as the scene unfolded in front of him. The neighbour probably thought that Dana was being hysterical, in fact. It was a result of the stress – or so it seemed to Henry, who was watching the action from his window, interested now, seeing how it was going.

The visit was cut short – the redhead was leaving. Surprisingly. Henry had expected that she would stay a few hours longer, as usual. He felt a slight twinge of disappointment.

He got back to the stove, not remembering he decided against the tea, unfocused. He decided to go outside to get some fresh new logs for the fire, before he forgot to do it, and he had to go outside in the dark, again.

One may suppose that he went outside just to meet with her.

But at that moment, it wasn't what Henry was thinking at all, and as if it had left his mind completely.

The marsh air was heavy but cold…which was refreshing in a way. He looked towards the water and as if for a moment he saw a figure, a woman's figure on the lake. She was made of shadows and fog, lost in the middle of nowhere. It had made no sense to him, just brought an eerie feeling.

So he was a bit startled and disturbed when *the redhead* appeared right in front of him. *She has left*, he had thought. But she hadn't – not quite.

A real life girl, not one he had probably imagined.

She saw him, too. Dana seemed to be different than she was just moments before, the smile wasn't on her face anymore. Her body was still, there was only this strange gleam in her eyes.

Slick hair without a hat was tucked firmly behind her ears.

She said hello, he the same...and then she decided to walk slowly to him.

She was on her way home, but she hadn't made it to the path just yet, so they had to run into each other.

What a day this would turn out to be for him.

She was moving toward him, hovering around him.

The first thing that came to Henry to say was:

"I heard about your cousin. I am sorry."

"What's there to be sorry about?" she said thoughtfully, and then more sourly, "If you didn't have anything to do with it."

"I am sorry about what your family and you are going through," he explained further.

She nodded and then said, "Thank you."

This overall business made him nervous, even though the police still hadn't questioned him. But they were slowly working toward it – he was sure.

He was not looking forward to that.

She was watching him attentively, still moving around, now with a slight smile on her face. He didn't know why he wasn't able to say anything else in the moment – *as if it is the first time he is seeing a girl, really.*

But on the other hand, it was obvious to him that she wanted to talk, and to hang around. That brought him a light feeling of pride. It seemed that Jonathan was not enough for her, his company... That was his opinion as well.

"So do you think she was murdered?" she asked to the point and out of the blue.

"I don't know," he answered, quickly and truthfully, taken aback by the question. "What do the police say?" he continued.

She sits herself on some logs.

"They don't know anything." They are now at the rear of the house, so Jonathan can't really see them from his place and windows.

Henry continues to go around his work, as planned.

But he feels that she wants to continue to spin out theories.

15

He should probably oblige.

She exclaims, "Do you think she is somewhere here in the woods?"

He doesn't know what to say – he pauses, but doesn't say anything. He slowly looks around to the not faraway trees, beyond the lake. They suddenly don't look as peaceful as they did a while ago. Clutching together tightly, as if holding a secret...

She looks in that direction too.

They are quiet. It is quiet. Just a shriek from an animal nearby comes their way.

"Let's go and take a look, shall we?" she suddenly said, excitedly jumping up to her toes. *Oh, this is crazy,* he thought to himself. But instantly, he got this tingly sensation running down his spine. As if he saw that this was what he was meant to be doing this afternoon. This was it, and he couldn't do anything about it.

She somehow had this way about her, making people do and feel things she wanted them to.

Henry was thinking, maybe a bit paranoid, was her actual behaviour now connected to him? To the one thing about him, that he tried so hard to keep a secret, hidden.

But not so well all the time. *It is always just simmering beneath the surface.* These last days here were filled with his so unusually vivid dreams and visions…surrounding all of him. *That might not have been a coincidence*, he thought, remembering the sensations he had been getting all morning. And then there was the gossip – about him, to be exact.

Could she know about it? He didn't really know.

Presumably she did, from other people, of course. In a town like this, and its vicinity, nobody could really keep anything just to themselves, now could they?

She may know it, because people around the town were probably talking about him already.

He just threw a sideways smirk, un-rattled, now wanting to get back to the practical side of things.

Not that he wants to change things all together, not really. What is meant to be is meant to be, right?

He moves closer to her and for the first time in this conversation looks straight at her – back to the theories.

"*So, she has gone missing. Does anybody think she has run away? Or do you think she was taken somewhere? Or that she somewhere has met a much worse fate…?*"

She is just staring at him, taking it all in, but there is no sound coming out of her slightly open mouth. She is taking in shallow breaths. She blinks with her lashes.

Then she continues with a slightly childish manner, set on to have her way, tenaciously.

"*Let's go look for her!*"

"*Into the woods? Now?*" *He raises his eyebrows slightly… questioningly, but trying not to offend her.*

"*Yes.*"

She is trying to excite him too, to get on board.

"*To what end? What good could it do us?*" *he sighs in exasperation.*

She steps out of their circle in the direction of the lakes and the woods further upon, dramatically, as if to make her point.

"She could be out there right now, asking for our help…" Again that gleam in her eyes.

He steps closer to her; them being almost side-by-side now.

She continues. "Or her body is decaying somewhere there, right now."

He lets out a quick breath, slightly surprised.

"Isn't that a job for the police?" he says in a matter-of-fact way, trailing off.

"We could help them out too, right now! They can't be everywhere at once," she says calmly now.

"The forests are huge…It could take them days."

"Exactly," she finished for him. "So let's start right now? Come on, let's go take a look – what is there to lose? Don't be so serious. Don't you want to see?"

She is right, she slowly got to him with all her oddly placed enthusiasm. He is curious.

The wind is still swaying around them, which is strangely comforting for him. The water from the ponds is slowly dripping. The logs of the freshly scented wood move around in his arms, and a few loose ones now fall on the ground.

He has a decision for her.

"Okay, let's do this, if that is what you wish for. Let's go into the woods together. To look, search…"

Now satisfied, Dana gives out a small purr, turning her back to him, she keeps on talking. "…Who knows, maybe we will find her, and we will be heroes."

She is already taking her steps towards the forest.

He turns back hastily, to go inside the house and get a different jacket.

Now he realises they haven't even said their proper introductions yet.

What an odd way to spend an afternoon.

But he believes that her heart is in the right place.

Chapter V

They were at it for a few hours, in the forest, stray branches and twigs crunching beneath their feet.

It was dark, damp, as if a light white fog was coming out of everywhere.

Henry pulled his jacket closer; he was starting to get cold. Dana's feet were skipping in front of him, always one in front of the other, like clockwork.

The trees were tall and majestic. Branches with needles on them made it all look almost festive. But in other parts of the woods, the trees were curiously as if dry. There were no paths as to speak of on the ground, they were just going were they felt like, and where their shoes were letting them.

It would all have indeed a beautiful and calming atmosphere, if only a stray ray of light would break through the trees and the blue sky would show through the darkness, for a little while.

But it couldn't, because the sky was greyish and all closed up, like it was here in this place at almost all times of the year.

Anticipating this, they had brought flashlights, so they could walk better, just in case.

Then it hit him – what a great place to hide a body.

She turned around and smiled at him, occasionally. It seemed the cold and damp, and the whole situation, was not getting to her. She seemed happy and light-hearted.

And a part of that mood was affecting him too. But only partly – for a different reason: a chance to see her smiling like that, in front of him…

But he did feel the dread.

"Did she come here a lot? Debra Lee, I mean."

She turned, surprised, maybe at the question or that he was asking at all.

"No." She didn't stop walking.

"Almost never," she elaborated, and then there was silence.

Then why would she think that they could even find her out here at all?

If Debra Lee didn't go here by herself, she could have ended up here not of her own volition.

So even he didn't ask no more.

They were looking around, under hedges, poking at things, into the small openings of the forest caves.

"Can you imagine, what if we found her...when no-one else can."

"No, I really can't." He was saying the truth.

She kept on rambling.

"...It would be like in all those movies, while two innocents are venturing through the woods..."

He reacted with a soft smile, then turned, perplexed, to the sound of a wild animal nearby. It was a bird, thankfully.

"...And then they find it. Shocking!" she continued with her thoughts, he didn't even hear all of it.

But then he jumped in. "But you are hoping to find her alive, aren't you?"

"Of course." She turned, and again she looked amazed, like a deer caught in the headlights, her eyes wide, eyebrows slightly lifted. "Of course. I am," she repeated. "What else?"

He decided not to pinpoint the obvious discrepancy between what they were doing and what she was saying.

She now looked deep into his eyes – waiting.

Her light-blue eyes were glistening, with specs of silver in them, the only light in the forest it seemed to him right now.

About at this moment, while being here with her, he was reminded of his dream, that feeling he had – fleeting, yet somehow still powerful for him.

For Dana, this was almost the first time she had turned to face him directly, as if she was afraid of him. With a strange man, in the middle of nowhere, the woods, maybe it wasn't the best idea.

And especially after what had most probably happened to Debra Lee, her cousin.

She shifted almost unnoticeably.

But she wasn't afraid – she didn't feel a reason to be after all.

He said while looking at her, "You are kind of odd, you know it?"

"Yes, of course" she answered, as if what else would he expect... But then a small hurt feeling shone through her eyes, as she was slowly turning to what seemed to be a part of a small path right in front of them.

She decides not to let it go: "You know, you are a one to talk – being cooped up in a strange cabin all the time."

She was probably right, but he had stopped hearing her this time...

Woooow.

Something had caught his attention, again, and he slowly lowered himself to the ground, kneeling down, suddenly exhausted. She was eyeing him with surprise, not knowing what to do.

He was acting as if he was searching for something on the ground, but in fact he felt sick, very weak. The feeling came over him again.

This is what he has been afraid of.

The situation, the disappearance, Debra Lee...getting under his skin again, like two nights ago when he had been led out of his cabin, by a force that was invisible to him, out onto the crossroads near their mansion, in the middle of nowhere. Thanks to what he had found there, just lying in the grass, the whole unexpected trip gave him a reward.

He must keep this out of his mind for now. She mustn't know, at least not yet.

There were the few secrets he was keeping from her, from Dana. And he would like to keep it that way. For his own safety most of all. Also, that he really didn't know what she, or anyone anyhow, would think about it if they knew what he had found – if they would believe him even. The way he found it.

He knew people, and usually they didn't.

When he didn't say anything, she kept going down the path, unalarmed.

He straightened up and continued after her, as if nothing had happened.

But he could feel she was a bit unsettled.

With all that drama, Dana suddenly allowed herself to let down her guard a bit.

She said now it a lighter tone, trying to lift the mood a bit:

"You know there could be some maniac living here in the woods, whoever…"

"If that is so, then we have no way of protecting…defending ourselves," he said soberly, as before.

They continued together for a while, aimlessly looking for clearer ways to get through the trees, being off the path again.

This can't go on for any much longer, he thought. He had to say something.

"Stop, stop, she is not here." It just came out, suddenly. Like he lost any control over it. He just had to say it.

But his sudden words were lost on her.

Again, she was leading upfront, talking almost to herself:

"You helping me, you know, it means a lot, that you care enough…I wouldn't be out here alone. I must help to find her." She sounded determined. He was surprised.

But then his words finally dawned on her, the thing that he said.

"Wait, what did you say?"

He felt the gentle breeze in his ears – in his mind – telling him that the forest was empty. Except for the animals, there was nothing here.

It was empty.

No Debra Lee.

Otherwise, he knew, he would feel it. Feel her.

Now he was sure, that this is why Dana decided to take him out on this little trip.

Precisely his powers: that was her unspoken reason. She must have heard about it, from someone. His alleged 'unnatural abilities'.

Witchcraft, some would say.

He was sure at that moment that in fact she knew. And had known, all the time. Or was he…?

Through his connection to her, to Dana, he had gotten himself in the middle of this whole thing, this whole mess. Connecting through her emotions to this drama…and this was the one thing he didn't want!

"What did you say?" she asked again. She was patient. "How do you know?" She was shocked by the situation but at the same time captivated by it.

Dana knew others had said he was psychic...or something like that.

That is the reason she asked him to join her.

But of course, she didn't know if she had believed it or not.

"She is not here. We won't find her," he answered simply, again. "There is no sense in looking for her now, you know. She is not here."

Each of them felt a small chill run down their spines. As if the cold finally got to them.

"She is still alive. And she is not here."

She took a small step toward him, a startled expression on her face, a question in her eyes.

But she says nothing.

She steps just a bit more closer now, light on her feet, on the tips of her toes, and plants a small kiss on his lips.

Kissing him! He knew, he just knew it! That he wasn't supposed to say anything to her. Getting himself all mixed up in this like that.

And it was not good for him, not at all, he knew that.

Now, because also he has too many – things – to hide, they will think about him too. One way or another.

Maybe that he had something to do with Debra Lee?

How could he stop it?

The woods and the onsetting darkness slowly embraced them, as they were set on finding their way back home.

Chapter VI

HE GOT INTO HIS CABIN, WHILE SHE CARRIED ON WALKING. Henry had sent her off on her way, and she headed home, not actually that far away. It was just a 10 to 15 minute walk with a brisk step along the pathway and bridges of the wetlands, even in the dim light.

The dusk had already engulfed his cabin, too.

He resisted the urge to put on a small lamp, so that he wouldn't be seen from outside. He didn't want Jonathan peeking in, or even thinking about what Henry had been doing so late out of doors. And he didn't want him to see what he was about to do next.

He just had to check.

He went slowly to his desk drawer, which was not the first thing on his mind, but still.

He was slightly shaking all over. He wasn't supposed to tell her that…anything, to tell her what he knew, that Debra Lee was not there, that she was alive. But somewhere else. Where, he could not know. Could not see, yet.

Even though it was true. Even though it may lift her spirits, who knows? But when this impulse came to him, he just didn't know how to control it.

Or at least he had to try really hard, and he didn't even want to stop most of the time. That is what made things so dangerous. He had no control over it. It was like he just had to show off!

He wanted to feel important. To feel…alive, really. Not just numb to all the things around him, the things that were alive and pulsing.

Pulsing through him.

Then there was his pride and vanity, knowing that he knew more than the other person standing next to him. There was power to it – that he knew he couldn't resist.

But he mustn't give in to it now.

Other people just might not understand; they never really do. And this could put him on all kinds of shaky, fiery ground.

This sensation, this overwhelming feeling of foreboding, happened to him a lot.

He was used to getting energies, vibes, that left him unsettled yet at the same time none the wiser. This was normal for him in the city – surrounded by people. There were so many people there! Lost or not lost yet – so many things going on.

But here in the wetlands? He came here to get some rest from this pressure, usually. Just to be himself, with his own thoughts, and unafraid of feelings that may arise. Or his 'powers' taking over all his thoughts…People in the city didn't take it very easily, or even act friendly – when it came to Henry's frequent change of mood, the strange emotions that came over him, or his outbursts.

When it began, he could never stop it.

He became overwhelmed, sometimes.

What a way to live! But it was his life. He wouldn't change it with anybody, he said to himself, but with a sad smile on his lips.

He could feel it even now, surges of electricity coming through his fingers – aw! When she passed by. That was unusual. He did get a bit rattled while seeing her anytime, Dana, a welcomed distraction in a slow day, but this was different. Something was happening around him, right now. And he was not bored.

But for this to be going on here, where there weren't people around – there must be something highly unusual going on. And there was, with the girl disappearing so suddenly…around him, somewhere near him.

Could it have something to do with the wetlands, probably?

Surrounding them all.

No wonder he felt it – trouble just always came looking his way.

And yet during this day it felt different to him – better in a way. He almost felt good about it. He felt a surge of excitement and looked out of his window into the dark.

He could always sense this, ever since he was growing out of a child's age into adulthood. He could feel the things around him – as living, in colours, always moving.

Sometimes even slightly before they happened. Some may call it intuition.

Then there were these dreams and visions – of places, people – some he knew, some he did not. Sometime they turned out to be important, sometime they did not.

Some might call him clairvoyant really...

Everything around him has its living, breathing energy – and in time, he had learned to influence it as well. But what he hadn't learnt was how to get something useful out of this insight!

Something for himself, in the chaos.

He was only just being overwhelmed, and that was it.

In the city, where he stayed most of the time, around people, he had felt that this slowed him down.

After a while, it started to be all a bit much for him – all the pretending and ignoring. Not being able to influence anything around him, really.

So he came here, to the wetlands. Maybe he will learn how to change things, improve them. Maybe it was time.

He reaches decisively now into the drawer, places his hand further back. The necklace is still there, the cool uneven brass beneath his fingertips.

He just found it laying on the grass, out there, not that far away.

Knowing it was hers – Debra Lee's. He was certain.

But who would believe him?

Chapter *VII*

THE NEXT DAY, THE WEATHER WAS BETTER.

She came knocking on his door.

The sun came up behind the greyish cloud for a while. The nature was abuzz, soft wind coming in with the smell of sea salt and decay.

The trees in the surrounding woods and around the path stood tall and majestic, as if unreachable and untouchable, but that is the way it always was. There were just a few passages that led safely into the opening in the woods and to the cabins by the lake. The ground there was firm and strong.

Only Henry was already outside, so Dana didn't have to knock. He startled her as he came around the back. "Please, please, help me. You've got to help me!"

He said nothing, unmoved. Just a slight smirk on his face.

"Now that we know that she is alive, it is even more important."

She went on and on...

"You believe me?" he asked her.

She was caught off guard with his question and didn't know what to say.

"Let the police do their job," he said simply.

"But the police aren't doing anything. I know you can help me. I believe you."

She said in a softer voice, "I can feel it."

Although he was moved by this vote of confidence, it was still not enough to break him.

He was surprised: why was she like that? So ready to believe in him, so easily.

Now he knew what he must do; he had to do it. It was necessary. He will not give out any more than he already did. Not unless he has to, so...he must send her away.

Let other people take care of their problems once in a while. He must protect himself first.

"Leave me alone, please Dana. Just go where you usually go," he hinted and turned his gaze to his neighbour's place.

He didn't want this getting into his dreams again.

She took that as a slight offence…as he knew she would…as if she prided herself that what she was doing was her own business, that nobody else should know about it.

Where she was going during her days or spending her nights.

She pouted her lips, then closed them altogether.

But there was a look in her eyes that this wasn't the last of it.

He will be hearing about this from her, soon.

He was glad.

She was really beautiful right now. As the smooth sunlight flickered on her lashes and brought up the almost real green in her eyes, a swirl came through her hair.

She turned softly, undramatically, on her heel and headed slowly toward Jonathan's neighbouring cabin.

Henry was watching her go. He should be feeling ecstatic now: free, satisfied…or at least relieved. He had got what he wanted.

He hadn't wavered one bit while saying no to her.

He was feeling lost instead.

Dana walked up to the small porch with the two steps, and then stopped right in front of the door.

She probably won't go in, she is thinking, she doesn't really feel like it.

Jonathan won't even know that she was here.

Suddenly the door sharply opens from inside. Jonathan steps out.

He was at the door, putting his coat on.

She is standing there, pondering what to do next.

They both stare at each other surprised.

Then Jonathan exclaims happily, yet formally: "Dana! It is so great to see you. What are doing here?"

She opens her mouth, but nothing comes out.

"It is okay. Come on in. I was just heading out. Please come in."

She moves reluctantly, still unsure.

"Hi. Well, if you were going out, I don't want to keep you."

"No, really…"

The conversation goes on for a while.

"No, wait," he said, trying to make her stay, "...we still have to make something of it."

He winks slightly, excited at the prospect of seeing her so unexpectedly.

She just shrugs, no, this is not what she is in the mood for, what she came for.

Henry is looking at them from the window, with the small binoculars he has by the windows – to watch birds as always, of course.

He has been watching them a few times now. He knew he shouldn't, but he just can't look away. Besides what else is there to do, almost alone in the woods?

And this is free theatre.

He sees Jonathan, looking all dressed up to go, happier as ever, gesticulating her towards the inside.

She is shaking her head unapologetically, hands in her pockets of the vest...scowling from the cold, a frown on her face.

Henry is watching her leave the cabin. She doesn't go in, leaving a surprised Jonathan standing on the doorstep.

Dana is on her way back, with a fast step, around his cabin, on her way home.

He secretly rejoices.

He is not for her, anyhow.

Chapter *VIII*

THE WIND WAS SWIRLING AGAIN, BLOWING THE WINDOW BLINDS OPEN AND CLOSED AGAIN. It was late at night.

He changed his mind. Henry was lying in his bed, but awake.

If she wanted Debra Lee, he would show her Debra Lee, or at least he would try. Show her cousin's last steps, her trail.

He decided he would go up to the mansion.

Right now. Dana's house. There was no time to waste.

If he fell asleep, and woke up in the morning, he would definitely change his mind again – lose the will.

He would go now, at night. Everything seemed softer, smoother, calm...As long as his resolve to get mixed up with them stayed with him.

To get mixed up with her, Dana; that was actually what he had wanted all along. That was what he couldn't stop thinking about this whole evening.

That afternoon, when she decided not to go over to Jonathan's cabin, to her lover, that had meant something to him, that had helped.

Maybe she really wanted to trust him, Henry. Trust him, instead of her lover?

What is the world coming to.

The time they had spent together the previous afternoon in the woods, maybe wasn't just a game to her – at least not in its entirety.

Chapter IX

THE TIME WAS NEARING MIDNIGHT. He walked fast. The night was starless. A flapping of wings rocketed up right above him. It was not a night to be walking alone.

But Henry knew the route up to the mansion well, even in the dark, because that was the way he went to his car when he wanted to get into town, or just away. The building was just close by, but in the opposite direction. He had always left his car parked here, conveniently by the path to the cabin – as close as it was possible to drive.

The rest of the way to the cabin, he had to go by foot.

Will she want to go with him?

He got to the house after 20 minutes at a brisk pace.

And what a house it was! More of a fortress, really. And now it seemed that even more than ever. Impenetrable, uninviting and standing all alone: menacing to strangers.

And yet one of its princesses, who had lived here her whole life (unlike Dana) had gone missing indeed ...

Thick concrete walls ran around it. It was lit, but there were enough places with darkness all around to help him.

He knew he must make no sound. Attract no attention to himself.

No guard dogs were to be awoken!

But he also knew this wasn't going to be a problem for him.

A walk through the park. It was all in the mind, and he knew his mind could do such powerful things to his surroundings.

He got over the wall...that was physical. His military training easily helped him with that. He put his mind to it, there was a slight surge of electricity – and all the alarms went offline, just like that.

He had done this before of course, but not on such a large scale – and in an unfamiliar place. With a lot riding on it. But he was not backing down. He was sure of his decision, his resolve. It felt easy, powerful. He motioned to the dogs on watch to be calm, instead of running toward him and barking…and they were.

They were happy to see him, started whimpering slightly, even though they didn't know him. And they lay on the ground and were still.

He was thankful, feeling the calm within himself as well. He was so grateful to have this special connection to animals; it made him feel alive just when it should.

It was so different.

There were some lights on in one of the windows.

He avoided the shafts of light that shone down from them as he walked beside the walls around the house, the soft, velvety grass sliding damp beneath his feet.

Now to find exactly where Dana's bedroom was, among all the other windows. He had come here with absolutely no idea. This is going to be embarrassing, when he woke up some old aunt. But he knew, or believed, that it would not happen to him. Just that was enough. He would be guided and he would find the way.

He was sure. This would be the next and hardest step. There was no room for error.

Out of all the windows, he chose one.

He was drawn to it, led to it, thinking strongly about what he wanted to accomplish and about her, and that was enough for him. Like everything he had done in the last couple of minutes. Better not to overthink it right now. He trembled a bit. But that was a good sign. He mustn't lose focus, not now.

He stood under the darkened window, which was on the upper floor.

This room was on the further side, a more secluded wing of the house. *Far from the main entrance. Facing directly only the woods. Just his good luck.*

He wondered what made her choose it, but there was no time to think about her.

He throws few small pebbles at the window.
Hoping he is right, and she is awake.
He is unalarmed, now unafraid.
He is probably not getting any more chances, this is it.

32

Chapter X

DANA JUMPED UP IN BED, WOKEN BY THE SUDDEN SOUND.

She was sure there was someone sitting by her bed. It had a familiar feel to it. *A girl, kneeling in fact. A sweet scent, coming to her, singing...* Adjusting to the darkness she saw there wasn't anyone, she was alone. She was perplexed what had woken her, now she heard it again.

Almost from the first moment, she was sure that it was some signal, meant for her. Something was going on.

It was the middle of the night.

She looked at the digital clock on her night table. It showed it was one hour after midnight.

Without hesitation, she showed her ruffled, not-yet deeply fallen asleep face out of the window, her loose hair falling in her eyes. She was gazing into the darkness.

There he stood underneath it, the clairvoyant, in the laser-like light of the serpent of the moon that suddenly came out above them, from behind the clouds.

It was quiet. There was a strange stillness to the night. Something – some common sounds – she would usually hear at this time, were missing. She was sure of it.

She just couldn't place what it was missing around her.

She must say to herself now that she isn't surprised on seeing him.

She had baited him to help her long enough. But to come here with such theatrics...

But it was him, Henry, at this time of the night, under her window.

He was in her space, her family's home, right now in the middle of the dark...

"What is happening?" she cried.

"Come on out!" he said.

"Why! Right now?"

"You wanted to go."

Looking for Debra Lee.

Then let's go.

"Now."

This will not wait for morning. Not for him. In daylight, everything was different, even the energy that he felt was always different.

"And bring your keys."

Well, she was coming out anyhow, she thought to herself, *who was she fooling?* She got dressed hastily, but warmly, and climbed out of the window. It was on the upper floor, but still she knew a way to do it.

Her feet touched the wet, thick grass in no time.

Henry watched as she climbed out of her bedroom window. The lamps in her room were switched off the whole time, and even with no light on, there she was suddenly on the ground next to him, in no time.

For this brief moment, he had admired her, without saying a thing.

She looked at him and felt the cold prickle of the night air on her skin. She also felt a not so delightful swirl of panic. She then smiled at him.

She was still painfully aware that it was silent all around – the guard dogs were not to be heard. Who knows where they were? When she looked, the usually blasting small red lights of the intruder alarm disrupting the walls around the property were off.

She followed him onwards. Her best foot forward.

"Come," Henry said, rather impatiently, without thinking.

Dana asked for this, this situation. Now she will see where it leads to.

This is not a time to be afraid.

With each step further on, it dawned upon her. The front gate seemed undisturbed. How did he get in?

She was afraid to, so she didn't ask.

He turned around to check on her, stopped a second, but continued then, eagerly to get away from the house as fast as possible.

He had this cool look around him, his face was undisturbed, and there was a certain sureness about what he was doing. He held out his hand – she took it.

He pulled her into the dark. He helped her to get over the wall.

"Where is your car?"

"I keep it outside the gates," Dana said.

Convenient.

"Okay, you do have the key? Let's take your car."

With each step further, she wants to see what he has to show her.

Chapter XI

SOMEHOW BEING IN HER OWN WARM CAR MADE HER FEEL SAFE.

As Dana rode off, from the house, the thickness of the night surrounded them as expected.

She held on to the steering wheel firmly. He would tell her where to go.

She looked over at him. His features in the soft light of the dashboard were still and calm and handsome, he was looking outside, concentrating. She drove them away from the house.

If he really was a psychic, or a witch – whatever – she wasn't going to ask.

She wasn't prepared for the answer, not just yet. What would she say? Would he even answer her?

No, this way she felt a little bit more in control…even though that was probably not true. At least she was prepared, thanks to her imagination, and she would see how it went.

Then it suddenly came to her clearly, again.

What if she was being completely stupid?

Leaving the house to go who knows where with a stranger like this.

Was this the way Debra Lee might have been feeling, the night she had disappeared?

A tremor shivered through her, and it was not only the cold this time.

Her hands started shaking slightly on the wheel. What if it was him?

What if this was exactly what Debra Lee had gone through? And could it be even the same stranger, the same one that she was putting all her faith into now.

And if so, she had gotten herself into a nice trap.

Lure her outside, and now kill her...The feeling of having her own car was just supposed to give a sense of false security!

She laughed at herself lightly. Even though she believed her panic was unnecessary, still she could not shake it off that easily.

Is she now walking in her cousin's footsteps, figuratively, perhaps even for real?

Had Debra Lee, who has been now missing for a few days already, felt helpless in the situation she had gotten herself into?

Or maybe she didn't even know.

They drove for some time longer, took a few bends, the headlights of her car cutting through the night. He told her to take a few turnings on the small country road.

She knew the man sitting next to her, yes, probably considered him her friend. But she had only had one proper conversation with him in all.

Maybe the noticeable hesitation to help her was just a way to lure her in?

What if he knew where her cousin was all along...

This road was almost always abandoned during the day, and even more so now, at night. Their whole surroundings seemed to be asleep, even she was getting a bit sleepy now.

There was a vast empty field ahead of them, with the forest line further beyond it, uphill – yet the vegetation here was already wild and soaring.

But there was something magical about the night around. She didn't want to turn back.

She will go on, wherever this leads her to.

Where is her sense for adventure?

Now he told her to stop by the side of the road.

The ongoing vibes were getting stronger. Dana had felt.

Was this a good...or bad sign?

Chapter XII

HENRY DIDN'T NOTICE HER DISTRESS. He was concentrating. He was lost in his own world. And even if he did, he wouldn't say anything.

He liked the night around them.

It helped him to concentrate, to hold on to his thoughts, even better. Better than in daylight, actually.

It was just a gentle veil. Not so much buzz around him.

He stole a quick glance at her.

Small rubies and diamonds dazzling on her fingers on the wheel. A modern design.

She had put on lipstick, a bit of makeup, he had noticed.

He wondered, when he had her all to himself like that: was it a last-minute thing, she had time to think of that, or had she gone to bed like that?

"Here, stop!" he said suddenly.

Just when she was starting to enjoy the ride...

The car crawled to a halt. He jumped out of the car, before she had a chance to even look around. The headlights were piercing through the darkness, illuminating what was in front of them. The most obvious.

They came to a bend on the road, nothing but grass all around. The road was still a dirt one. Her house was not more than ten minutes away by car.

She jumped out of the car as well. Pulled her coat closer to her body.

"This is where she was taken," he said.

What a desolate place it was at night.

"Are you sure? And where is she now, what happened? Can you sense it?"

"I don't know." He really didn't, not just yet.

He had been to this place before. The day after Debra Lee was taken. He just had to stop here, coming from town that evening. He had already heard about the disappearance. His head had suddenly started to blur, and it hurt. So he got out of the car, stumbled. This is where he found her necklace. It just caught his eye in the near wet grass.

Like it was waiting for him.

The vision, of Debra Lee having it on her neck – and then it being torn off – came to him. Her lovely face turning around towards him, then surprise in them, as the bright lights were flashing in her eyes, being the same night-time around her as well.

But he wasn't prepared to tell her cousin Dana all that, not yet...

She came nearer to him. He had forgotten about her completely for a while.

This was the place where the necklace came off Debra Lee's neck. Here is where she stood, in horror?

"So you have been here before?" Dana asked.

"Yes. Just after it happened," he said truthfully.

Then, after a slight pause, she went on:

"And have you told the police...about this place?"

"No. What would I have told them?" there was disdain in his voice. He looked at her.

"And you can...sense it?" she asked carefully.

He nodded, unable to say a word, looking down at the dark ground. He kneeled towards it, carefully.

It was enough for Dana, for now.

Henry was moved somehow by this display of trust. She was able to see that it was all a struggle for him.

"And you can follow the trail...to where she was afterwards?"

"I don't know...I...maybe. We will try," he said curtly, but then shot her a quick look. Just to check how she is taking it all.

Or maybe she is still here, Dana thought to herself. A short quiver passed through her.

She got into the mood to get back into the car. It was getting cold. Instead she stood still.

But the previous tension was gone. As if something that made the night so terrifying had moved on, at least for now.

In the shining headlights of the car, she kneeled next to him. He asked,

"And why you are doing this – looking for Debra Lee – anyway?"

He went on watching her.

Dana said, "Because of my mother. She wants that." Her voice was very quiet, while she was saying that.

That kind of made sense to him, although he didn't understand why…

So it was not just her morbid curiosity about the situation. There was an underlying reason. Dana got up, got more into the spirit, to be playing detective now.

"So this is where she was…this is where she was taken. Probably in the dark. Must have been on her way home. She screamed…He must have taken her into the car." Their home could have just as easily been reached by foot from here. Even from the town, only it was a longer jaunt.

Dana spun on her feet toward him.

He was watching her still, his eyes wide with amazement.

"I don't know," he just said again.

She moved around a bit more, ferociously.

Looking for something they have missed.

He laughed. "You are really into it."

She repeated his laugh in her reply. "Don't make fun of me! You are as well."

"No, I am not! Only to help you. Aren't you afraid?"

She said eagerly, "Are you?"

"No," he replied.

It was almost unbelievable how happy they could be in a dreadful moment like this.

"Let's go then," he said.

"Where are we going?"

"You drive."

"Let me think," he added after a while.

She drove off into the night again, leaving that forsaken place behind them.

He hadn't told her about the necklace.

Henry still believed that it was one of the things he should keep to himself.

He navigated her through the woodland roads, into the nearest town.

They were there in no more than another ten minutes.

He made her stop in front of a shop window on the main street. All the sudden lights of the bright street had blinded them. The shops were quiet now, closed and dark. The street was wide, abandoned at night, as it was after two o'clock. But all was well lit. The stores were the classic ones for shopping in this type of town – they were near a watch repairer, antiques, a goldsmiths…

Nothing stood out for Dana.

"What was Debra Lee doing that day? Do you know?" Henry asked when they were parked, with a good view of the street. "Do you think she was here?"

"Yes, they believe she had been to town. The police are onto it. Nobody knows what she had been up to that day. They are trying to put it together. But nobody knows for sure anyhow, not yet."

They had lost sense of time for a while, it all slid by so carelessly.

"I hadn't seen her that day," she added, after a pause.

They sat for a while. Nothing much was happening. They didn't know exactly what they were waiting for. They were stiff and silent, none of them even shifting.

Not one person passed by. The bars were also already closed in a town like this.

Just one un-soothed cat shrieked into the night.

She hadn't been to the town this late before. She hadn't had a reason to.

It all seemed so calm.

They talked a bit, exchanged a few pleasantries, but nothing too factual. She had got him to smile at her a few times. But she noticed when he was putting his attention to her, he was somehow losing his concentration on the big picture – Debra Lee, and why they were here…

She could have got out of the car, to investigate more…but she just didn't feel safe enough.

"Has the trail gone cold?"

"I don't know." He tried to think, to catch the drift again, the flow of the feeling, the connection to it.

But when he put his mind to it, there were just echoes of voices, lights.

He didn't like what he saw. He closed his eyes.

Nothing tangible – nothing he could hold on to. It just made him nervous.

"Whoever connected was here, they are probably not here anymore. Let's drive some more," he said.

They got out of town again. Somehow the emptiness of the countryside seemed peaceful to Dana.

But it seemed it wasn't meant to last for long.

"Turn up here," he said.

His head was starting to hurt. That was not good.

He was definitely on to something.

"Stop the car!"

"Here?" She drove onto the side of the road and turned off the engine.

If he just wanted to get out of the car to get a breath of air or they are at the place they were headed to, she didn't really know.

In the darkness, there was a small steep rounded hill in front of them.

He started out the climb, moving uphill.

She followed him with a fresh step, the flashlight from the glove compartment of her car in hand.

They made it to the top in not a long time. There were no trees on this hill, just simple grass, which made their climb much easier.

A view of the great part of the valley opened up to them, even in the dark.

The wind was fast and brisk up here.

She snuggled her collar closer to her chin and lips.

He didn't seem cold at all – buttons on his coat and shirt wide open.

He heard the screams, the agony…the fire, breaking wood.

You could see the whole wide countryside from up here, even the town nearby.

No, this was from another time.

"What's happening? Are you alright?"

"No, this is not right. Not what we are looking for. This is from another place."

The shrieks and the screams, cold in the night, it would not stop.

"Let's get out of here. This was a mistake. I am sorry. Let's go home," he tells her.

They hear the distant tolling of a church bell even though there is no church in sight, and especially not to be heard this time of night...

Then she saw her, a woman weeping softly, head facing the ground. The sound was carrying in the air.

And Dana had a sudden feeling of eyes on her, staring intently, as if there were others... their faces turning towards them, disrupted from a long-sleep. *Did he feel them too?*

He probably did, because Henry grabbed her hand and pulled her down-hill. They continued with their descent rather quickly. She didn't say anything, her lips pressed together. *Was this place an ancient burial ground?* came to her mind. *Or what he meant by what he said*, she was wondering. *Ding-dong.*

Or something even worse? ...gallows?

Maybe she didn't want to know, and it seemed he didn't want to talk about it either.

At that instant, Dana realised the meaning was that there are even deeper horrors buried also in history – no need to look for it only in the present day.

Yet, for her the place had a strange energy to it; it was alive even at this time of night.

Wisps of fog were slowly coming up from the valley, covering their feet.

Thanks to the wind, a few stars shone through in the skies above them. You could feel the morning was getting closer, but it was still pitch black.

It was nearing four in the morning.

Anyhow, she was sure she had experienced something special, and she wouldn't have wanted it any other way. If it was any other case, she wouldn't even believe it, but this – this was different. Tonight made her see things around her differently.

But this still was only a feeling she had, nothing tangible – just by being with him, she wished only if he could let her see more, what he saw, as well!

While being confused and cold, she forgot she wasn't supposed to be heading for the passenger's seat. It was her car in fact.

He was standing by the other side of the car, waiting, watching her.

Now she had felt her own keys in her pocket.

44

There was this semi-wild look in his eyes he tried to hide, when the light of the car went on and illuminated him, while she was unlocking it.

They switched their places.

Once they got into the car, it would be better, she thought.

They closed the doors. The soft glow of the dashboard was calming. The tension was gone.

Whatever was out there, it was not in here with them.

She drove. She was almost sure of the way.

He was looking at her, watching her now. Not lost in his own thoughts, as before.

He was probably wondering what she was thinking.

"I would like to see what you see" she said to him, as if answering his thoughts.

"You would not, believe me" he said to her, more curtly then he intended.

She was pale, her lips tightly together once again, hands trembling slightly on the wheel.

"How are you feeling?" he asked.

"I'm okay, going to be better. I am just tired, and the cold is getting to me."

"Better go and get some sleep. Let's get you home. Back to your bed."

She smiled, starting to feel a bit different.

"What was it back there?"

"I am sorry, nothing to do with Debra Lee. Forget about it... Just some old vibrations. I cannot always be sure..." He didn't finish the sentence, looking out of the window.

"So you are still on for looking for her, even after this?" there was a higher pitch to his voice.

He probably meant knowing what all it could entail.

"Yes! Yes." She was sure.

Knowing that not only her cousin, but also her own livelihood, future and finances might be depending on it, she added: "...of course."

"...You are really strange, again," he just concluded.

"I am? How about you?" she exclaimed, but in a playful tone.

A smile was playing on his lips.

He was feeling happy.

He knew he was successful in what he wanted to achieve.

He had showed her he was just not a nobody, that he was somebody.

Somebody special.

He knew that she knew that by now.

She parked near the mansion. This was where she usually left her car, so nobody really saw into her business.

There was no-one around. Just peace and quiet.

A bird called out.

She felt for the keys for the main entrance in her pocket, slightly shaking with fatigue. She was hoping she wouldn't wake anybody from their sleep.

It was easy for her to forget why she was outside at this moment, at this hour. Not just after a late-night date with a boy, that had gone on almost until the morning…

Debra Lee, her problems and everything surrounding her was gone as in a wave.

But like every wave, it comes crashing back.

Then they got out of the car. They were outside again.

Again complete strangers in fact.

A crash of her fear returns again. What was he, and what is the suspense surrounding him? Is this the right path for her or not?

He would walk back to his cabin on foot, in the dark; there was no other way there.

"It is no problem," he said confidently. "Good night. Have a good rest."

She couldn't help it but to call out after him:

"Is there something more?"

"I don't *know*."

"But there must be…" her words trailing off.

A flashlight flickered and she could see him no more.

It was time for her to go home, back into the house.

Chapter XIII

Her mother, Sheryl, told Dana that everything was fine.

She was fearless. Like she usually was.

She told Dana this is the way for them.

They talked the next day, after Dana's midnight trip.

Her mother told her to call him again, but this time to ask him around to the house.

Her mother had heard about this young man and his special insight into things. Around town, she always had her ear to the secret grapevine. That is how she knows things.

She always did.

"This is how we survive," Sheryl said.

Now that they were without Dana's father, things had got a lot more difficult. And possibly they could get a lot worse, financially…Without her father, it turned out that they were not so welcome in his family either.

That was often the way that these old-traditional families and their views went.

"We could get an extra step ahead using this boy. Don't be afraid. I will talk to him. Call him to the house. Make sure nobody except Theresa sees him," Sheryl mentioned the maid. "I will take care of the rest." She smoothed her blonde-perfect hair back behind her ear and onto her back. Her blue eyes, which were similar to Dana's, but much more intense in colour, sparkled.

Dana did as her mother told her. She didn't want to; she didn't want to beg for anything and especially not from him. She called him after lunchtime. He was to come into the house late that afternoon.

Chapter XIV

HER MOTHER PROBABLY BELIEVED IN HIS ABILITY, HIS POWER. *She will see for herself, she is saying.* Especially after what Dana told her had happened last night and in the afternoon before that, in the woods.

Her mother was not backing down before anything like this – the supernatural. If it proved it could be useful to her, she believed in it. Sheryl was sure that even if a part of this worked, it belonged here. It had its place here amongst them, on this planet.

So, when it manifested itself in a form of one the neighbours, she was fine with it.

Anything to prove her to be useful to her husband's family, in their search for Debra Lee.

And not many other similar opportunities presented themselves to her.

Dana wasn't so sure.

She feared that it wasn't something that they could control, and that it could end up swallowing them whole.

She could already feel it happening to her, in a way…she was worried.

Chapter XV

HENRY WAS GETTING DRESSED. He had to look good. He had finally been invited, into a house like this.

He had to play the part correctly. Just the blue cashmere sweater, or even a silk tie?

He must look his best.

He knew he belonged there.

Only the others must believe it too.

He was nervous coming to his not so large mirror in the bathroom. This was the most time he had spent looking in the mirror in the cabin, maybe in all the time he had spent down here.

Usually he just wore wool, something warm, a bland neutral colour, to keep the cold out and so he could go out easily.

He was leaning forward uneasily, with the necklace in his hands.

He was afraid that by holding on to it like this, he might break it.

Debra Lee's necklace.

The one he had found on the crossroads.

The one he hadn't shown to Dana.

The one he had found the day before when he had apparently been led to that place, all of a sudden.

There was no way to explain how he knew that it was hers, Debra Lee's.

It could have been anyone's.

But he knew.

The other day he had felt that she was alive, while searching for her in the woods.

When he put his mind to it, he just knew.

Now he tried feeling that signal again, to hold onto it, but he wasn't sure.

He closed his eyes, but he couldn't reach it; he felt nothing.

Maybe because he was not relaxed at all.

This was what it was doing to him. This whole outing.

He felt anxious.

Suspicious even.

What if they had called him in order to lure him into the big house…so that the police could search his cabin?

And what if they found this: an object that belonged to the missing girl?

What if Dana has already been suspicious of him since they met and told them about him?

He could hide it in his hiding space beneath the floor, under a loose floorboard. He went to do it. But if they discovered the necklace during the search…it would make it seem even worse.

He just found it during his walk in the woods, lying there on the ground.

But then why hide it so meticulously?

That's what they would ask.

He would have no way to explain that.

He would not take it to the house with him. It was true that he was tempted to show it to them, the mother and the daughter, so that they knew that he was for real.

To prove to them that he was indeed what he said he was.

Whatever that was.

But then the ladies of the mansion would know that he had Debra Lee's necklace…They would recognise it easily and implicate him in a crime he had not committed. Then they would probably find a picture where she is wearing it, to prove it was hers. Of that he was sure.

It was a specific necklace, not to be mistaken for anything else.

Joyful looking almost.

Even when he touched it, he could feel that.

He would put it in his mother's jewellery box, which was full of unusual, left behind trinkets.

But he tried to follow the police logic: if he knew it wasn't his mother's, because he found it outside, and far away, why would he put it there?

He would leave it where it was. In his study desk in the middle of the room, near the door. But he wouldn't push it back into the furthest corner of the long drawer, where it has been until now.

He would put it in the front of the drawer, so it was visible almost immediately.

Nothing to hide. He found it, then just left it there, and then it was forgotten.

Nothing important at all.

On the other hand, he knew that at the house the necklace would help him – a lot. It would help him draw the connection to Debra Lee.

And he needed help with that.

This was just what will be needed, he thought to himself.

He looked in the mirror one last time. He combed through his hair. He looked good. He was satisfied. Just about ready to get out the door and lock up.

Standing on the porch, he unlocked the door one last time, walked back into his room, opened the desk drawer and put the necklace into his pocket.

Where he is going, he will be needing it.

That was of the most importance right now.

The thing was delicate.

It was two brass wings joined by a bright-blue stone in the middle, which changed its colour when you moved it. It was iridescent, opal-like.

It was nothing…inexpensive, he was sure of it.

Such a small thing and what a lot of worry and trouble it was causing him!

Chapter XVI

THE HOUSE WAS HUGE. It gave the appearance of many different styles combined together. The modernist, cubist shapes of the building dominated.

It had two storeys in some parts and three in others, with a flat roof that in good weather was probably used as a balcony.

There was the magnificent antique-style main entrance door, with a knocker in the shape of two lion heads instead of a common bell. The whole property was surrounded by a huge beige-coloured wall.

It was almost ugly. It was more like a prison. Henry couldn't understand how anyone could live here. The antique heads of lions of the front door clashed with the whole style of the house, but added to the pompousness of it, and probably to the people living there.

It is possible everything was for the added sense of security, being in such a remote area.

There was the rear service entrance as well, with the terrace steps facing the deep woods and then across a patio were doors, which led straight through to one of the living rooms.

He was led there by one of the maids, and then through a service door to another wing of the house. She was probably instructed not to take him through the main entrance hall and to keep him out of sight of anybody as much as possible, he felt.

On the other hand, he was sure Dana's mother could have had visitors brought up to the house, without it arousing much… suspicion.

Then he was taken into another room, a living room, where he was set to wait.

But the ladies were already there.

Chapter XVII

THE LIVING ROOM WAS GOLDEN. Just as he had imagined. There was a cosy atmosphere, soft carpets and gilded sofas.

The centrepiece was a fireplace, with marble columns. The lamps were jade-coloured and matched nicely to what he presumed were original Chinese vases.

With no windows to be seen, it seemed as though the room was in the centre of the building.

Everything was lit by a soft light. Even the pieces of art hanging on the walls, oil landscapes of foreign countryside scenes, with sheep and streams, had a light upon them.

This seemed to be their domain.

This is where they appeared to be at home.

An exquisite tea set rested on a low table, already prepared, with a wisp of steam coming from the teapot.

They both watched him with attentive eagle eyes.

But this was what he was prepared for.

Chapter XVIII

Dana was standing near the fireplace, her mother seated by the tea.

It was the first time Henry had met her mother, Sheryl.

She extended her hand, as she got up from the sofa and greeted him nicely. She was polite, in control. From their brief conversation, he understood that she wanted him here, and probably in fact it had been her idea.

That meant she must believe in his abilities: that was good.

Perhaps her situation was too complex for him to understand, and that's why she felt a pressing need to turn to him for guidance at this moment.

"Thank you very much for coming." Her coral-painted lips were smiling.

Dana's demeanour was a different story. She was just watching, quiet. Her eyes fixed on him.

The blood in her veins was boiling, anger rising.

She didn't know how she felt about having him in the house.

She believed in the cause, as her mother had told her to, but still she didn't need to be happy about it. To have him here, now, in her living room seemed too personal to her. Like he was invading a part of her she didn't want him to see. Opening up to him, in this way!

Sure, Henry is such an odd and interesting character, one she was okay to talk to while on the outside, in the wetlands...but now?

Even though he was attractive and all, she didn't like it.

He sensed her mood.

He mustn't get riled up by her or get into an argument.

He mustn't get pulled into this, even though he just as easily wants to.

He must keep in mind the reason he came here.

He was civilised.

But he couldn't take his eyes off her.

She was beautiful.

Dressed in a red dotted skirt, with a flowing hem ending just above her knees, opaque white stockings and Mary-Jane heels.

Her blouse was cream, with a high neckline ending with a gleaming honey collar, set with rhinestones. Everything was properly buttoned up.

The stones were throwing reflections all around the room and onto her face…fiery silky red hair which was framing it ended in a rich wave just above her shoulders. She had kept it just out of her face, to show off her lovely contours to her best advantage.

She was dressed almost as a schoolgirl, extravagant, but with enough fashion sense to pull it off.

And it suited her very well.

Very different from how he had been used to seeing her in the marshes – yet here she was, in her natural element. Yet underneath still the same girl.

Sheryl had noticed the way he was looking at her right away. She didn't say anything, what she thought about it she kept to herself. Nevertheless, being herself, she was probably already making a note in her head how she could use his apparent infatuation with her daughter to her benefit.

Mother and daughter both had the same eyes – but the mother's eyes were deep icy cold, and they were watching him calmly and calculatingly. Unlike Dana who had fire in her blue eyes, or at least when she was watching him. The cloudy grey always moving, changing from light to darker tones: like in his dreams.

"Of course, thank you for inviting me." He was looking around the room.

The mother, dressed in a soft peach-coloured skirt suit that was also proper and fitting, said, "My daughter told me that you would be able to help with the situation."

He didn't say anything.

He was still suspicious about all their intentions.

The vision of the police searching his rooms came back to his mind at that point.

"Yes."

"I of course believe in your abilities; you don't have to doubt that," she continued.

By hearing that, Henry was surprised.

Where does both their sureness of him come from?

Was it just desperation on their part, resulting in their making themselves believe it, wishful thinking?

"Of course, we – I would need more from you. We would need you to find Debra Lee."

A pause mid-sentence, for a greater effect.

"Tell us what you know. Or what you are able to share with us."

Dana smirked a little. She was obviously not so convinced. And something was making her nervous.

He must find out what it was.

Her mother was still leading this, steering the helm.

Chapter XIX

"BUT I DON'T WANT TO BE DRAGGED INTO THIS. If I find anything…" Henry looked at Dana "…then from that moment on, I don't want to have to do *nothing* about it. That is up to you."

"Yes, we can agree on that. We will make sure that nobody knows about your involvement. If this is what you really want."

He nodded in agreement.

"Have the police talked to you already?" the mother inquired.

"Yes, they did. They didn't seem to want anything more."

Dana was thinking that must have happened in the morning. Yesterday he had said nothing of the sort.

He continued: "That is what I want. Not have to discuss anything in this matter with the police."

The p o l i c e. The light necklace burned in his pocket.

"We will show you Debra Lee's room."

Now the mother was in control again.

He was quiet.

"Something is just not quite right." He turned his back away from them, to relieve the tension he was feeling.

Sheryl was thinking of a way to reassure him.

He continued. "Why do you want to find her so much? And why use…me?"

He looked over at Dana, again.

He remembered what she had said yesterday about Debra Lee. That she wasn't necessarily her favourite cousin, not at all.

Dana couldn't stand it any longer, she cracked under pressure… First a smirk and then. "Yes Mother, why? If we find her, then she will just be back at the house…Believe me, it is better here without her," she said, with a touch of theatrics, to an invisible audience.

Her mother rolled her eyes at Dana with a quiet sense of disbelief, but wasn't in fact acting surprised.

Then Sheryl smiled at him, shifting slightly on her sofa.

Good thing she didn't try to sugar-coat this to him in any sense.

"You are probably right. Your sense is correct," Sheryl told him. "We should probably talk about this some more," she continued in a politician's voice, not prepared to take in any failure.

"You are not of pure heart," he blurted out.

Henry was trying to pinpoint the vision that was suddenly coming to him, the one that gave him such uncertainty. He just said what he had felt in that moment.

As if it was important, he was just suddenly realising.

It was not that easy, it kept sliding away.

Henry turned around back to face the fireplace. The given tension in the room had gone up, almost to a simmering point.

Maybe their intention toward Debra Lee and her wellbeing was not as straightforward as it would seem, from an observer's perspective... *What do they really want from him? And what do they want for her? Or is it just for themselves?*

Yet Dana's mother's expression remained calm despite it. She lifted her chin slightly upward, her blonde hair falling back.

They both stared at him, as if caught in a lie. He now had managed to catch them off guard. This seemed to hit them where it hurts. A wave of emotion came over him.

"You didn't even like her. You hate her. You said that yourself!" Henry was thinking aloud.

He was glad that at that moment he had shone a light on this inconsistency; he felt he was in fact gaining points with them. He didn't stop there:

"So why look for her? Why me? Why go to such lengths? Why go to all that trouble?"

He was waiting, unsure if they will even ever move.

Sheryl got up, brushing her hand over her skirt attentively.

"We are in financial difficulties...at the moment," she said simply – as if it was self-explanatory, as if nothing else was needed. And of course, it wasn't.

She continued. "Ever since my husband left. He left us with almost nothing."

Now he was a little bit ashamed to be prying into their private business. But at least they knew he was observant.

Dana gave Henry a long look.

Her mother continued, her voice trailing off "…he left for Europe. With some young woman. Just like that. Before he left, he effectively severed all his ties with his family, and the business… They are not happy about it. A scandal, they might say." She coughed slightly: "If they wanted to." She raised her eyebrow, as if to confirm they were in agreement.

Dana looked at Henry again, turning her glare from her navy Mary-Jane shoes up to him.

He took his time to take in what he had just heard.

He was listening intently to her mother.

He heard a sound of slight rain from outside.

But then realising moments later the room had no windows, it was probably just a feeling he was receiving.

A feeling of sadness. Abandonment.

"He left us and forced us to turn to his family. To try to get into their good graces again. You see…Well, it has proved to be rather difficult. I wasn't very well liked or welcomed by the family at first. I was very young. I had to fight for it," Sheryl said.

He must admit, she was still an admirably beautiful woman, even now.

Long days ago beauty queen. The lips, skin glowing, hips swaying…but that was just a memory.

Dana moved to the furthest away corner of the room – the living room was huge of course – as if she was leaving her mother to finish this conversation in private.

When he then looked over at Dana, he realised the mother must have had her baby girl very young.

"And there is Dana's trust fund, of course, but that is still about two years away…"

The daughter turned – she had obviously heard – and wriggled her nose as if uncomfortable that her mother would talk about it – and he looked straight back at her.

It was possible that some of the hostility he had felt from Dana may have not been directed toward him as such, it was just an outcome of this whole situation surrounding her – Debra Lee, her family, her mother.

The thought made him feel suddenly warmer; the coolness of the room that he had felt previously was gone.

In fact, he felt uncomfortably warm now…And then he felt the burning sensation again, in his pocket.

Debra Lee's necklace.

He loosened an extra button on his white shirt, which he had decided to wear underneath his fine lightweight blue cashmere sweater. Now he felt a bit better. He looked down at his elegant brown shoes, which he had had to polish again after the hike, before he visited the mansion. They shone.

He weighed all the new information in his head. Facing the fireplace now, his face turned away from them. Henry didn't feel the need to say something about what her mother had just confided in him.

And they for sure weren't waiting for this, his personal thoughts on the situation.

Dana had returned back to them now.

He thought about men in dark blue, surrounding his house… But that was just his imagination.

He must think about himself – about this situation and how it affected him.

He would be the perfect suspect: he lived alone, so there was no one to verify his whereabouts; it was an isolated place in the woods, and he had a reputation as someone strange, mysterious. He would be perfect for it.

At least in the movies.

Such a rich family as themselves, they didn't care about who took the fall in the end or care about the people around them for that matter.

But he considered himself smart enough, and most importantly capable enough, to accomplish what they said they wanted, what they thought they needed. Was it worth it, though, for him to get involved in this?

He was playing slightly with the necklace in his pocket.

But he is not just a person, who doesn't fit in anywhere he goes. And now somebody really wants him, needs him.

As Dana moved slightly closer to them, by the fireplace, her perfume hit him.

He glanced sideways at her, noticing that she had on a lot of makeup now; her eyes painted. Lips and lashes – she looked so different from the girl he had been used to seeing in the marshland.

He remembered he already was part of the events.

They both were.

A slight hint of a different scent came to him, he didn't know from where, a heavy and intense one. As though from roses, it was an uneasy feeling; he shook it off.

He turned, definitely and firmly, on his heels, to face them.

"It doesn't matter." He was sure of his power.

Nothing could stop him. There were no obstructions in his path.

Harrowing roses…

He knew he wasn't leaving this house today to be only a half-missed opportunity for them – as a nobody.

Because he is somebody.

It was easy for him to prove it, whenever he wanted to.

His hunger to feel something, connect to something different, from a different place…was just there.

And if this fact, combined with his pride, got him in trouble, so be it.

"For this – for what I do – to work, you don't have to have a clean heart. It has no bearing."

No matter what their aim was, whether it was entirely selfless, or even just partly. Even if they didn't care for her, and were being deceitful.

He took Debra Lee's necklace out of his pocket.

"Take me to her room. This is hers. She was wearing it the night she disappeared. I found it on the crossroads. It will help now."

The necklace of course took them by surprise. "In the place I have shown you" – he turned to Dana – "in the fields. Out on the wet grass."

They startled a bit, swayed into motion to go on to do as he says. They led him to her room.

A small parrot sitting in a silvery cage at the back of the room suddenly announced its presence by squawking loudly three times.

As if he had not drawn enough attention to himself, the red-green creature then began to mimic Henry softly. "Take me to her room! Take me to her room.

Chapter **XX**

HENRY ENTERED THE ROOM. Dana didn't want to join them.

She disappeared further up the short hall, dimly lit. Probably gone to her own room; he didn't know.

Her mother was waiting outside Debra Lee's room, guarding the door, so nobody would see him go in the room. Or even just down the hall of the house, so there would be no unnecessary questions.

The room embraced him.

But it was not cold, nor warm, nothing really. He put on the light to see better. It was her bedroom, closet and adjacent bathroom.

Nothing too big really, or even fancy, but a nice place for a young girl to grow up in.

He walked around, touched a few things.

The décor was: cosy.

Everything well-matched, nothing stood out that much.

Light and dark browns, caramel colours, on the bed and so on. A small dressing table with a mirror.

A box of cheap jewellery.

He looked into the bathroom, which was clean, quiet.

It was tidy, the tiles were cold. It didn't seem to him that the police had been there that much. At least not on a first look.

It appeared that was it. Debra Lee. She wasn't like Dana – he would never expect to see her cousin Debra Lee near the cabins, or in the marshes. She was just not like that. Not likely to go wandering there.

So nothing much to connect her to that place.

The mother was shifting nervously in front of the door. She peeked in once or twice, to see his progress.

He held the necklace softly in his palm.

Her cousin had recognised it – and said that Debra Lee had worn it around her neck. Just as he presumed – a valued piece of jewellery. Now it was finally confirmed to him.

He didn't see anything, he felt nothing.

Not until…Dana barged into the room.

Chapter *XXI*

THE ATMOSPHERE CHANGED VEHEMENTLY. At first, he couldn't believe how different the two cousins seemed to be.

Dana was like a breeze of fresh air, though no, not that...more like fire to him. She started touching things and they came alive.

She was impatient and excited...wanted to see for herself what was happening.

And wanted to check on him, of course, as well.

What a disruptive force on the whole situation she proved to be.

The tension in the room had risen. The lights started flickering slightly, to his eyes, not enough for the girl to see.

Henry went into the bathroom. There he saw it. He saw her: Debra Lee.

She seemed to him to be a carefree girl, and possibly always had been. Not like her cousin, who was probably up in her face all the time.

Her thoughts were simple, her feelings were simple, he sensed. As was her lifestyle...that explained a lot about the room to him. Just all the things a youngish girl of her age would need, to look good...and nothing much else.

Now Dana's mother was angry at her that she had barged in like that, disrupting the concentration of the moment.

But she was firm on guarding at the door, and so she stepped back into the hall.

They were in the bathroom now, alone, the two of them. He turned to Dana.

"She was different then you."

"Yes, of course," she said, not knowing what more to say, waiting for instructions.

"Simpler," he said, trying to reach out for something.

He continued. "Didn't dress up that much." He was looking at her, moved his eyes to the hem of her skirt, the red circles on white silk, just where her thighs were showing.

"Yes!" she was catching on. "More like brown...mouse, I would say..."

She then finished her thought with a new sentence. "But everybody loved her for it. She didn't put much effort into anything. Or thought for that matter. In my view."

Henry frowned at her words, but he didn't say anything.

Debra Lee didn't feel any danger in her bones, or so it would seem.

She ventured only into places she knew, only did things that she liked. Or learned to like the things she had to do. She wasn't that open to the vast world around her.

She wasn't even that curious about exploring it.

Going into the opening in the wetlands would have seemed beneath her. Why would she do it, anytime of the day, when she could be sitting in the Main Street café, gossiping with her girlfriends? There it was nice, warm, and proper.

Why...change anything?

This came to him in pictures, all of it. In feelings, emotions as well. He could feel it, like Debra Lee had. It was just a brief moment for him, but this was the way she had felt all her life. Now a new vision came. A more up-to-date one, suddenly, as he had wanted. As all of them wanted.

He supported himself on the frame of the door, back in the reality of the bathroom.

Now he spoke: "But something was different that night. She was different."

He came to the sink, now frantically touching at the things there. Bottles, makeup – which started falling into the sink.

"She was putting makeup on. Lots of it. Like you."

He turned to her again.

"That's not like her at all...You are right!"

She blushed lightly, smiled with her lips and eyes softly at him.

That he even noticed her at all.

Her face.

Her mother couldn't stand it no more.

As she heard the commotion, Sheryl closed the hall door behind her and came inside to join them.

She was standing now next to her daughter.

"She was going out. Meeting someone...Some man. A date," he said.

He continued with a question: "Do they know where she was headed that night?"

"I don't know. But they didn't even know that she wasn't home that night. The family doesn't know. They really don't tell us anything. I don't know. The police – I don't think they do, either," Sheryl said.

"It's an older man. She felt important. Secretive. And..." He was perplexed he couldn't find the word. The word was dirty. As if she knew she was meeting someone she shouldn't, that the others, her parents, would be against it. Shocked.

Debra Lee grimaced to herself, into the mirror...

But he wasn't really sure they would like to hear that. So Henry didn't say anything.

But he saw on their perplexed faces that they sensed what he meant.

"I don't know. I can't think who Debra Lee could have been meeting that evening," Dana said slowly. She seemed confused, as if in a daze.

Her mother watched on.

Then Dana said with a sense of urgency,

"And who might he be? Is he from town? Is he the one that took her?"

Henry felt that the connection with Debra Lee was lost.

He just saw her fantasy of that night and the preparations.

But he saw nothing of the night itself.

Both the women standing next to him were breathless.

Sheryl was the first to appear to get back to reality. She took a careful leap toward him.

"You must help us, you must. To find her, I mean."

They were all in the bedroom now. Then she said less pleadingly, back to being the one in control:

"I believe that you have a gift. Dana and I both believe it." She looked at her daughter.

Dana just coyly looked at the ground.

Henry was happy to hear that she included her daughter in her statement.

"Use this gift, help us with it. Don't leave just as this, clueless as they are. I plead with you."

The gentle breeze coming from the wetlands, all the way from the sea, was sweetly buzzing in his ears.

He felt he had changed his mind. He was thinking, getting ready to say no.

"No way, lady, I want nothing to do with this." This was why he went to the cottage! Into the wilderness, to get away from it all.

To get away from people like this, to get away from troubles like this!

Problems like Debra Lee might be having right now…or not. Maybe she just ran away. And it had nothing to do with him – people who would just like to use him and then publicly humiliate him, take away his secret.

He told them that.

To get away, away from the darkness, of that opening up right in front of him…whenever he chose to do so.

Her mother answered him, "I would do anything. Get you anything you please, anything you wish."

Dana was surprised when she saw her mother being deadly serious.

"This would get us back into the favour of the family if they could see that we had helped. We'd be welcomed again."

If he found Debra Lee well and alive, for that matter, Henry was thinking while hearing this…But he didn't say that out loud, not just yet. Instead he exclaimed, not in control of his sense really any more:

"Why would I do this voluntarily? Get myself tangled into it! You don't even know if she is alive."

What if they find her dead?

It was all bubbling up:

"No, to make myself go through this. For what?"

Why were they even talking to him – why didn't they talk to the real authorities if they were so invested? He felt this altogether can't be good.

He was upset. He said it like they had nothing they could offer him – Nothing such a rich family could offer him at all in exchange for his services, not knowing what circumstances he was getting himself into, with Debra Lee...

"Anything you would want. Anything that you need," Sheryl said. "I will pay the price," she offered, continuing.

This was getting too melodramatic for Henry's taste. But he went with it.

They believed him, because he had told Dana while they were back in the woods, that the girl was alive, Henry realised.

Why not get involved then? What did he have to lose? So why not ask for something for himself, even something that might be considered strangely...extravagant.

There was only one thing in the room that he wanted.

For himself, anyway.

Decision made, he went on to answer her question. "Her."

He looked straight at Dana. "You could offer me her."

Chapter *XXII*

Dana w4as just taken aback by this, unsurprisingly shocked.

Terrified, really. She stood with her mouth slightly open, unable to move for the moment, especially when she realised her mother was seriously thinking about it. And in Dana's mind, her mother still held the power to decide everything for her, meaning she became even more terrified.

She was perplexed, as if finally...all attention shone on her.

She was unhidden.

It was all she wanted in a way.

But like this?

She was suddenly exposed. *More important than Debra Lee... more than her own mother.*

But probably: still a prey to him, Henry, this mysterious neighbour.

But still in her heart, she was moved slightly, that he would care for her, want her, all just so easily!

Wow.

Without even knowing her that much, not at all. Or so she had thought.

Deep in her thoughts, she was missing the opportunity to speak up in time.

Henry went on. "With no complications for me, I'd need a proper introduction to the family and the elders...no questions about who I am, my wealth, my place in society. No prenuptial agreements. Just a glowing introduction and recommendation to the grandfather. All nice, simple and easy."

A different kind of quiet then settled on the room.

There is nothing more he could want from them.

What could they offer him – money? They maybe even didn't have that, at the moment.

But h e r, he could find use for her, what to do with her. She would have been like a seized exotic butterfly.

Just for him, for him to keep. For him to get to know, learn how to get on with her. He would have liked that.

It would be a nice fantasy, wouldn't it? He knew he wanted a bit too much of them, that they weren't on good terms with others now anyway.

But why not take advantage of the situation...if he wanted to?

He had a feeling that everything new he was likely to see connected to Debra Lee wouldn't be nice.

She was missing, from her own home, after all.

Did he want to open himself to that kind of torture? To go through it alone, or even with Dana at his side?

Of course, Debra Lee might still be alive, he thought to himself.

The mother slowly nodded. "Okay!" If it meant getting back their status, their place in the family, and money and wealth, it was probably worth it.

"This is the only thing you could offer me to get me even further into this mess, otherwise I go home now and forget this wretched thing all together," he continued.

"But only if you succeed – with what we are looking for. Finding Debra Lee, and then getting our rightful position back. Not telling about this to anybody, not a soul."

How simple it was for Sheryl, offering her daughter like that. *As a prize. To a complete stranger.* But she almost knew this moment was coming; as soon as she saw him walk through that door, she felt it in her bones. This was such an unusual thing to ask for, but so be it. It wouldn't come to it, anyhow. Her daughter had a mind of her own, she knew that.

Even though they were a bit on shaky ground now.

"Of course." He understood the endgame, to which it was all leading to, and he was okay with it. Whether he would find Debra Lee alive or dead, he was afraid to add that to it.

At this, the mother took a step closer.

"Okay, we are agreed."

She wasn't about to lose this opportunity to get what they wanted, not if it could be done. And apparently so easily, or so he made it seem.

He sighed; a bit relieved. He wasn't really expecting she would be okay with this in the end. But if she agreed, that is so; this gave him extra motivation to get to work.

Dana was just looking at the whole scene, amazed, as if it had nothing to do with her.

Chapter XXIII

THE NEXT DAY, DANA HAD NOW A NEW CHALLENGE ON HER MIND.

At home, at the house, the atmosphere was not too pleasant. She needed to get outside.

Her thoughts now took her out of the wilderness of the woods to the town, to the moderately busy streets.

She was sitting at the driving seat of her own car, and she was anxious. *Alone. Playing with her fingers on the steering wheel of the car.*

She couldn't quite let it go. What was Debra Lee up to that day? Where was she headed? And why hadn't she got home?

There were many such small details that kept popping into her mind, small conversations she used to share with her cousin. She was trying to remember, but really, she couldn't.

She just wasn't paying enough attention the first time around.

Who was this mystery man that Debra Lee was meeting?

What was she really like anyway?

What were her desires?

She just didn't know. Not enough to help her in any way anyhow, which she now regretted.

How come the police hadn't found anything yet? At least that is what the police had told them, and the officers hadn't given them any information. Not even about her mystery date.

Could it be someone from the school, a classmate or one of the teachers?

It might sound simple, but that could just as well be it, because it had a sinister ring to it. Something you would be likely to hide from others. In her mind, her fantasy kept working in overdrive.

She would go to Debra Lee's school, to find out something more from her schoolmates. She was her cousin after all, so she had a legitimate reason to try and ask questions, to worry.

Right now she was looking at the front windows of the shops, the ones she had been watching with Henry a few evenings back, in the small, yet busy, downtown...

Could Debra Lee have stumbled on upon a crime here...here!

Who knows? Why not? The town was quite a busy connection point to the other, bigger cities, with the highway nearby.

Even that was possible.

She eyed the storefronts suspiciously.

Yet still she was coming back to him, to Henry. What he had said to her, here, the other day.

And to his recent talk with her mother.

That he wanted her – in exchange for procuring his services.

She was sure she was unable to face him right now. Not just yet. Could she imagine? Her...a married woman?

Still, there was a lot of confusion about this in her mind.

Oh my.

Yet it was appealing in its own way. It would give her a chance to get out of these heavy relationships, away from her family – she was old enough. It could be the freedom she wanted, to stand on her own.

Be her own person.

But how did he know, that is what she would desire?

Yet she also came back to the roses, the harrowing roses by the moors. She didn't know why.

It was as though they had a hold on her, trying to tell her something.

She would much rather be there, right next to the wetlands, not here now.

As if the vision of the roses, their existence, was there to remind her that she was not quite part of it – of all these things around her, the town. They seemed to be tying it all, and her, to that one place where the roses grew.

A place that didn't seem significant right now.

As though she was under a spell, spellbound by them.

She kept thinking about all these things she had experienced with him over the past few days, and how she felt. The sensations were repulsive to her body yet inviting at the same time. And they are not going to let her go that easily.

74

Even when she tried to apply a practical solution to the problem, take a look at the situation in a sensible way, as she was doing now, it was still there.

As if the grip of these other things around her was getting tighter.

There wouldn't be any simple solution.

She shook a little bit with cold, looking outside intently, now at the reappearing afternoon rain.

Still, she was looking forward to talking to Henry, talking to him soon.

But for today, this is a mission for herself, herself alone.

She drove off to the school, which Debra Lee attended this year.

Chapter XXIV

HE WAS RESTLESS. What had he got himself into again? The cold water of the raindrops was dripping behind his collar and onto his neck. Otherwise there was no sound. Henry got into his car to escape the unpleasantness outside.

He knew that if he put his mind to it, he could really do it.

He could find her. He knew that he could.

He was angry.

With all this, with the terror around, in people's hearts, and the ugliness that he was a witness to. But in the end, he was really drawn to it. He just couldn't let it go. It was a part of him. At least it was now.

And it had not been before. For a brief moment, he tried to remember how it was before, but couldn't really. When he was younger, more innocent, without a clue of this world of things that was about to open right up in front of him.

But no, really…he loved it.

He knew that, in his soul. It was right for him.

It was what made him who he was – in time. It was the one thing he was sure of. And the one thing that was his! (What the others can't see, they can't take away from him.) Where he had felt safe. Despite how intangible it was.

How bizarre this was.

Even though it made him feel so sick at times.

With the visions, dreams and all these emotions.

Only she, Dana, had now put it under a different light. She acknowledged it as a part of him and this made him feel different.

But on the other hand, she was a part of it now too. She was a part of his dreams and visions, a maze and whirlpool of unfocused wild emotions in his head. So it somehow stayed the same, but was it all the same or has it changed?

How wonderfully great that made him feel.

The feeling, exactly what he has been looking for...How could she have known that that was what he wanted?

As if she looked at him and immediately knew him, it seemed it would be possible for her to accept him, just as he was. With all the darkness she had in herself as well. Her fascination and her love of the wetlands and more, he was sure...

But who knows, maybe he was wrong...maybe she wouldn't be so accepting of him when it came to it, who knew? Maybe she was even scared of him now.

Then what he must do is to prove his worth to her. And start by making good on his end of the bargain – the promise that he had made to locate Debra Lee, once and for all.

The shadows and the cloudiness of his sweet yet bitter dreams of Dana overcame him.

The vague feeling of importance of it all, for his future.

That their connection isn't just his illusion.

But what did this have to do with Debra Lee? He was in his car. He drove past the place he found the necklace the night after she went missing. As if the birds were singing that day and leading him only in this direction.

Now the birds were all quiet.

He got out. It seemed like they were just watching him intently from the trees.

This is where she was taken, Debra Lee.

He was holding on to the necklace, hidden away in his jacket.

It was giving off some kind of heat.

He must not think, think too much. He knew that.

Just go with the flow, let himself to be led.

He got back into the vehicle and the next thing he knew, he was parked on the main shopping street in town.

The setting of the dark outside was starting.

The streetlights were already on, even though the sky was still visible, darkening to a black-blue dusk.

He had stopped in the same place. Again. He gazed along the row of shops, with the occasional apartment windows up above.

This was the place. He just knew this was the place.

Where Debra Lee was.

She was alive. His heart rate was pumping.

But she was not entirely all right...he could feel that.

He just needed to be sure and to know what to do next.

Please help me.

Sitting there in his car, waiting for something to happen, everything in his surroundings seemed to slow down again.

Other shop owners were closing up and going home, one by one. The lights in the stores started to go out.

Then something happened.

The antique shop owner was coming out of the shop. He was closing for the night. He was an older man, grey and scrawny looking, a type you wouldn't notice that much. He collected the advertising board and then went back inside to take the precious items for sale out of the window.

Henry's car was parked right in front of the shop, only on the other side of the street, so he could see him quite clearly.

The old man closed the metal shutters, but he stayed inside the shop...He locked himself inside.

He didn't go home.

He must have an apartment there as well, Henry thought.

Things around him stopped making sense.

He could hear faraway voices and screams from the gallows on the hill, from long ago.

Confused, he held his head in his hands.

He heard laughter - a girl giggling. He would swear there were a couple of girlfriends in the street, sharing secrets, no care in the world. But as he lifted his gaze the street was empty. Yet he could still hear it.

Then he saw - a figure, as if dancing in the street, through the parts of the light and shadows, not stopping for anyone. As if *she* was made out of...fog and the wind, yet the skirts were still swaying.

He leaned forward, because this got his attention.

The vision was gone.

A close-by lamp started blinking and the metal shutters on the opposite shop were rattling fiercely, *as if they were never going to stop.*

Henry knew, right there and then, that Debra Lee was in that building. He was keeping her there.

She was there. It has meant something, something big. That is why he was drawn to this place from the beginning; it made sense. He knew that without any doubt whatsoever.

As he had always suspected he would, if he could put his mind to it, with the correct motivation.

Underground. In the basement?

In a dark room.

His head hurt.

He was thinking now. What he was he supposed to do next?

Going in there on his own wasn't a good idea. And he wouldn't even know what to do if he did go in.

He didn't want to get mixed up in it. He should go to the police. Of course. What would he even say to them?

Then he knew what he must do.

As he promised. They made a deal.

He must go to Debra Lee's and her family's home right now, at night.

He was calm and composed.

Chapter *XXV*

SHERYL RECEIVED HIM IMMEDIATELY. Henry seemed composed and was well dressed.

But when she looked into his eyes, they told another story.

The feelings of those involved were now a blur – all he could see were the images. He heard a creaking door. A beam of light through a keyhole. An antique watch. And a candle, burning.

Sheryl knew she should brace herself, her hand firmly gripping the sofa.

They were in her drawing room; in the part of the house she was using now.

It has been a little over 24 hours since she had last seen him.

His eyes were open wide, wild and sparkling in the dim-light evening lighting of the room. If she didn't know better, she would be a bit afraid of him now.

But when he spoke his voice sounded calm, as if cold. In control, unexcited.

She was hoping, praying, he was here with some good news to tell her.

He was now leaning over the fireplace in the middle of the room, looking in the fire, which was now lit to keep the night cold out. His favourite place in the room, it seemed. She was sitting in a loosened position on the sofa, on its silver-gold cushions, as if unsure what is to come next.

He turned to her:

"I have found her. I know where she is."

She released her breath. Even his face seemed to change now, to soften up a bit, with this revelation.

She didn't know why, but in that moment she felt sorry for him.

As if the other things on her mind suddenly moved into the background.

To her surprise, she realised that he had taken quite a hold on her, in the very short time she had known him.

She had enough bad emotions of her own, enough not to be interested in taking on the ones of others.

Then all her other more pressing feelings rushed back.

"And where is she?" she whispered, her voice breaking at the end. "You must tell me now," she added with more authority, but still softly, just in case he should want to wriggle out of it.

"I will show…I will tell you," he kept on shakily.

He seated himself on a sofa, at a right angle to hers, his hands on his knees.

"I will tell you. But nobody else. It will have nothing to do with me. I know where she is…but don't ask me how." His composure was back now. "But I know," he added definitively.

"I was led to the same place again, the one I visited with your daughter. You will not tell anyone where you got this information. How you deal with this obstacle is up to you; it's your problem to handle." This was as they agreed previously.

He told her all about the antique shop, its owner, the space downstairs. He told Sheryl that he believed it was the shopkeeper who took Debra Lee. Again, he emphasised that it was up to Sheryl to decide how to tell all this to the police when she told them where to look for the girl. Explaining how she got this information, how she knew, would be up to her and her ingenuity. He himself wouldn't know how to explain it to them anyhow.

Sheryl's well-manicured nails and golden ring clicked on the glass coffee table as she was getting up.

Dana was nowhere to be seen.

They shook hands on it. She agreed. They had a deal.

On the terms he had insisted on earlier.

Now he delivered his end of the bargain.

Dana's mother was not afraid, she would handle this from now on, she told him. No need for him to worry.

She let him out of the door.

All the questions, suspicions, unpleasantness, she will take up on herself.

He was thankful.

She watched him leaving into the dark night, for a brief moment.

Otherwise – she had work to do.

Chapter *XXVI*

It all happened so suddenly. Suddenly it was done.

It was big news.

Debra Lee was back home.

She was okay, healthy, but of course in shock. They had found her in town. She was in the hospital for a short while.

At home it was buzzing, everyone was talking about it. Nurses, police, her closest family – it was all just a blur.

Nobody paid much of any attention to Dana.

They just smiled, held her arm with a warm hand for a short while, said variations of "Don't worry, she is going to be okay" and walked off.

Dana wasn't really worried, just confused about what had happened. In such a short period of time, such a big change.

She went back to her room alone.

Of course, they didn't let her to see Debra Lee yet.

She imagined they felt it should just be immediate family. Debra Lee was still weak, they had told her. So, it was difficult for her to believe she was really there, back in the house now.

Dana had put a few pieces together by then: her cousin had been found in the basement of one of the shops on the main shopping street. She was held there as hostage for a couple of days. Her kidnapper was an older gentleman, one you wouldn't really even notice in the street, the owner of the antique shop.

He was shot dead during the scuffle of the rescue.

So they didn't have the chance to get any information from him.

She was found by the police; they had received a tip. An anonymous one? She didn't know.

It was a pity that nobody had a chance to talk to the owner of the shop.

Had Debra Lee been kidnapped for ransom? Nobody has asked for one...

As Dana heard more, while walking through the kitchen and all areas of the house, it seemed it was all done for sexual favours probably...or it seemed that way to her now, in regard to how everybody else was acting.

They said Debra Lee was healthy. Unharmed. But was she harmed in some other way? They didn't say, and she didn't know.

Dana realised she hadn't seen her mother for quite some time. She was with the police.

She found Sheryl later in her rooms.

This is what the police told her:

"The kidnapper was not the man Debra Lee had been on the 'secret' date with."

On the way to drop her home, they had got into an argument. In the heat of the argument, she got out of her date's car in the middle of nowhere, at a crossroads not even very far from the house. She could have easily walked home from there.

The bright lights of the car headlights are shining.

She jumped out of the car, had a bit to drink. It was dark everywhere.

He left her there.

Then another headlight followed – another car appeared. It was the kidnapper; he must have been following them from the restaurant.

He mostly has been jealous, presumably.

He'd had his eye on her for quite some time.

At first, he stopped the car to help Debra Lee, but then...

She remembered nothing, just that a long time later, she woke up in a dark place tied down, on her own. With a bump on her head.

When Dana then asked her mother what was going on after that, Sheryl didn't know; she said it was all a blur to her cousin... They didn't tell her mother more.

Chapter XXVII

THEN HER MOTHER TOLD HER THAT SHE HAD BEEN THE ONE WHO TOLD THE POLICE WHERE TO LOOK.

Henry had been there to see her early the previous evening. He had told her. Sheryl then simply followed her gut what to do with what he had told her.

Dana was wondering where was she at that time, when he had gone to see her mother alone.

She couldn't believe it at all, what her mother was telling her:

"I told the police where to look for her. Told them I had remembered what Debra Lee had said to me about a shop owner, and that she was afraid of him…and they just went with it."

Dana was slightly in shock. "Don't worry," she heard again. "Everything is okay now. It is handled."

The rocks of ice in her mother's whiskey chimed. Her mother got up, with a slightly kittenish, satisfied smile hidden on her face.

Dana shivered unnoticeably, as an unknown terror got under her skin. Her eyes wide open.

Her mother told her again: how he came here, what he told her, how he knew.

"He finished his part of the bargain; he came through." She was happy. "This is just the thing, the miracle we needed…and it all worked. All is forgotten now, with the family. We will be okay now."

Dana walked around the house. And she felt it – the change in the atmosphere.

They were all thankful to her mother. Thankful to her. They admired them both. They were in awe of them.

Where she went, doors almost opened themselves in front of her.

The people working around the house, the police sergeants… greeting her.

This has in a great way lifted her spirits.

But a vague feeling of the unknown and of not understanding how it happened remained within her.

She felt the need to speak to him, to Henry, soon.

She was sure she will. She must.

During the next two days, her mother reported everything back to her, as her grandfather continued talking to Sheryl.

All of Dana's father's sins were forgotten, as far as it affected them anyway. Her grandparent's son, her father, had run away from them, left them with no knowledge of his whereabouts or anything about him. How was that even possible? She couldn't comprehend.

Her grandparents had never liked her mother; she was a party girl, a dancer, and they were almost entirely against their marriage. While they lived in the city, her father had never really kept in touch all those years. He said he didn't need them. He had made a quite a lot of money on his own.

This is how the story appeared in their daughter Dana's eyes.

So now, coming back to them, her mother wasn't entirely sure of what their position would be. What was the future for both of them – her and her daughter?

But she, Dana, was her grandfather's own blood – his own blood!

Reminiscing, Dana was sure Mother would find a way to remind him of that. They were welcomed, or at least tolerated, under his roof, but still in a precarious position. Their money back home almost ran out. So they came here, to the wetlands, *to the family home.* To her uncle and aunts, but they had been met with a lot of unasked questions and raised eyebrows.

When her father left, some few months ago, he hadn't even contacted his family: he was not in touch with them, or her and her mother. He just left them. He didn't even call to explain, so they didn't know either…It was just not like him at all. Even though their little family unit never came out to the wetlands to visit the family there that much – just a few trips up there for holidays – still her father always kept in touch, at least with his parents. So they always knew what he was up to.

Now they were all just surrounded by doubts. The only thing they knew about him now was that he was all right, safe. That message he did relay to them, not to worry. But that was all.

Now Grandfather had promised them everything.

All worked out as her mother had wanted to, as she hoped for.

They had a few small talks, Grandfather and Mother, the day that Debra Lee was found and since then.

Dana's trust fund from them…was intact.

If they wanted, Grandfather would arrange that some smaller sum will be released now, at her will and disposal, he will do that.

And he will take care of their house costs, living standards, of course.

They will provide for all.

"You, Sheryl and Dana, are of course a cherished and un-expendable part of the family," in his own words.

They were all taken care of now.

Chapter *XXVIII*

DANA TALKED TO HIM BRIEFLY. The next day, outside, near the gates of her house.

Henry was on the way to the wetlands, to his cabin.

They will talk more tonight; he said he will come for her.

She was wanted back at the house, for a joint meal.

Later, the night was quite lovely. The air was getting warmer. A shining half-moon was hanging on the blue-black sky. Its light gave an unnatural sheen to everything, as if the garden had come alive.

She was getting ready for bed, she was really tired today but remained in her clothes.

She woke up from light sleep a little while later. The rest of the house seemed to have gone to sleep. It was quiet. It was a little after 11.

She looked out of the window. She put on a warmer coat over her.

He was waiting downstairs, pebbles announcing his arrival.

They were driving in his car.

"How do you that – get into the house, past the alarms?"

"Happy?" he asked seemingly on a different topic.

"And why do you do that?" she frowned.

He didn't like her questions very much.

Henry knew he shouldn't do that. Drawing attention to himself, by not drawing attention to himself (how ironic!). The house had gone quiet; the otherwise always watchful dogs were suddenly sleeping.

But he couldn't help himself...

He was feeling bold, self-confident, and he wanted that to be noticed. He remained unafraid.

Finding Debra Lee did that to him.

He hoped Dana would handle it as well and be unafraid of him.

But he knew there was always a possibility that it wouldn't be like that...

"Debra Lee is back at the house." The slow humming of the car seemed to have returned her thoughts to matters at hand. "They had found her in the town. She was returned to us. She is alive and well."

She said it in a slow monotone voice, sounding like she had presumed that he didn't know. But beneath her voice still lay a confusion; a disbelief of that this has really happened.

"I know," he said heavily, as if worried about what she would say next.

Then a slight pause.

Henry began laughing softly. And his guest slowly joined him as well. The tension between them was broken. All the anxiety they were going through was gently soothed away.

He was watching the road ahead of them.

She moved in her seat a bit and turned toward him, leaning in, eyes alive with mischief again.

"I wouldn't have believed it. Only two days ago – only two days ago, we were driving here in the same car."

"Actually that was your car." He turned his face to her.

"I know. You know what I mean! It is almost unbelievable. We did it. We made it happen!"

He slowed and stopped the car.

As if this was what he had been waiting for. *For her to be excited.*

Waiting for the tension between them to be dealt with, changing into excitement. It all seemed to make him so distraught that he couldn't keep on handling the car at the same time anymore. He had to stop.

He turned to her.

The car halted by an empty field, on the side of the road. The lights of the car were still on.

They kept on talking for a while.

The moonlight was bright around them, so they could also see each other pretty well.

"I am sorry, I didn't..." He tried to apologise.

She started saying something, but he interrupted. "I didn't know what to...I went straight to your mother. Didn't want to get you involved in it...any more than necessary, anyhow."

Psychic ability. How awesome was that. She would say that to him now.

And then:

"It is okay, I understand."

That made him calmer.

Chapter XXIX

"...IT'S OKAY, I UNDERSTAND," DANA REPEATED, TRYING TO SOOTHE HIM. "Of course, it was necessary. To speak to Mother about it. And how did you know, how did you find out, where she was?"

"I don't know, I just did," he replied.

"Just like that? And it was all connected to the place that we had been to together, just a few days before."

"Well, not JUST like that."

"I can't even imagine what she went through. Unbelievable. Like in a thriller!"

Henry smiled sadly, didn't really know what to say to that.

She looked at him attentively, shifting her whole attention to him.

He was glad that she did. She let out a sigh.

"I am just glad. Glad that we did it."

He slowly leaned toward her, as if unsure it would be welcome.

He softly touched a loose strand of her hair and put it behind her ear.

They talked some more, about different things, for about half an hour and then he took her home.

She had felt the energy around them, it was almost palpable.

Imagine! He had had psychic powers, his whole life...she would envy that.

All seemed to glisten back home. The milk-white marble of the steps, the mirrors reflecting when she turned on the light in the hallway. On the consoles were arrays of white plush roses, delivered as a celebration of Debra Lee's return. As a symbol of her innocence... Suddenly Dana glanced at a reflection in the mirror – the roses turned scarlet, decaying. *As if dripping of blood.* She blinked, and they were gone. The reflection was again pure white, her own skin porcelain.

She hurried back into her own room.

There was the clicking sound of her heels on spaces where the floor was not covered in high carpeting. She caught herself reflecting in the mirror, looking and almost not even recognising herself.

The change in the house was distinctive, it was almost beautiful now.

She saw him a few times in the upcoming days.

They met near the house and drove off to the fields, near the town, never back to the wetlands, not yet anyhow.

He told her a bit more about his visions, and she was fascinated to hear about it.

Amazed really. Of course, he was still careful.

She told him about the change of the atmosphere in the house, how everything was going now that Debra Lee was back. How Grandfather was now in favour of them and he promised that their position will be restored.

So all was right, all was fine.

"Mother got what she wanted, what she had set out to do."

"And you, I hope," he added, smiling shyly.

"Well..." she was wondering, "I think what I want is still different." He continued looking at her.

"More wild," she added with mocked theatrics.

Now Henry laughed, looking down.

They hadn't talked about the 'deal' Mother had made with him, not yet anyhow. It seemed to be more of a burden for her – and her influence on the family, now that he had finished his mission.

As if in this moment, it didn't mean anything much.

Yet it gave a strange sheen and glitter to their interactions from then onward.

He used his energy, his insights, pretty much draining him in the process, she was sure of that, even though he didn't let on – and Debra Lee was home.

Now, as far as she and her mother were concerned, it felt as though they were finally wanted at the house, as a result of their positive involvement. As if they were finally noticed for the first time. They were grateful for that to him. Now of course his request was very daring, if nothing else, uncommon...but that made it even more so mysterious, so that she couldn't take her mind off it.

It was as though he was saying they should skip the few years of courting, and she would be his from this moment on...forever?

Henry was not pushing anything forward, or even reminding her of it – as if he almost had forgotten it himself.

Of course there was nothing more he could really say to her. He had said his part.

Their connection, attraction, was there as well, present all the time.

Of course, it remained hidden beneath every one of the conversations they had.

But there was another side to it as well.

Their relationship was volatile.

At times it would all be fine and calm, then in an instant, they would descend into a place filled with tension, drama and anger.

They could just as easily snarl at and hate each other as they did before.

Even though it was exciting, it was tiring as well.

And no one really knew where all this intensity came from.

He felt that even with her wild side, it was still not enough for him, he was not satisfied, and he will never be. It was just not enough.

He always needed more from her. It was just not enough.

Oh, how she wanted to ease herself into this relationship.

She felt quite eager. How nice would that be? Even though it definitely wouldn't be easy.

There would be fireworks and lightning for sure.

As if it would be hard for both of them, but necessary for them at the same time...that they had found themselves in one another, in a sense. *They are unexpectedly compatible...*But in a way that was their own.

So eager yet so shy from the outside world. As if they wanted to live on rules of their own.

But she also started to have thoughts, angrily, about: *Who is he? And does she want to let him to limit her freedom?*

She felt that her calm, that she had felt these few days after Debra Lee was found, still connected with everything happening before, was slowly being lost. And she was starting feeling as she did before, wild and unpredictable. Unsatisfied.

Chapter XXX

BUT FEELINGS OF GROWING SUSPICIONS, FEAR AND DOUBTS…STARTED TO SURFACE.

What if Henry found Debra Lee some other way?

What if he was in on it the whole time?

Dana did occupy her mind with those thoughts, just for fun, at first.

Made a few wild versions about how it could have all gone down.

This was probably where all the anger was coming from, the tension, between them.

Then one morning she told what she was thinking to Mother, while eating breakfast toast, in a lighter tone. But as she said it out loud, it suddenly took on a life of its own.

As if it was all remotely possible…as if it made sense…!

Her mother was very dismissive at first, not believing that any of it could be like that, but it slowly started sinking into her mind as well. Henry as a criminal in all this?

The police didn't find the old man's accomplice after all, and he probably had one, but only was out to be proven now.

All these thoughts also brought with themselves a feeling of fear, of worrying. And of respect towards him…but also of an altogether uncertainty.

Sometimes there was this wild, cold and almost self-destructive look in Henry's eyes – was this to be overlooked?

Henry knew these feelings could surface within the women; he was aware of that and he had told them that it was a possibility before.

This was the effect he had on people, in the end. That is why he didn't want to tell them about his abilities, help them, why he didn't want to open up to people! Just hide. In plain sight. So people didn't go turning against him in the end, as they always did…in a very intense way.

A hint of something unnatural, paranormal, surrounding him always.

Was Dana like everybody else, driven into a corner by something she didn't understand? Was she not open enough to the bigger things in her life, like things of faith? Unaccepting of change; wasn't she the one that needed to change a bit?

Or just to trust him more and believe her instincts?

And even with all the positive, intense feelings she had been experiencing with him in the last few days, Dana started falling into a slightly paranoid state.

What if it was all a game for him?

He seemed to know a bit more than other people, about many things.

What was that really like?

Unapproachable, godlike and controlling – but still with this strange affection, obsession, tenderness toward her and to her needs.

But still it all seemed so exciting in her eyes.

And what if she is just a fool to him? Ouch. And even if he was such a cunning criminal…Would she still want him?

Could something so amazing – like finding in him something that she actually needed – really be happening to her?

In the midst of the most perfectly hellish situation, that she could even imagine, around them.

Just a rich girl conned by a good-looking conman.

Or was she with these thoughts being just untrusting and meantime killing something that was worthy of her time?

Is this just the way that wealthy people think and react when they suspect that someone may want and be after them purely for their money or their fortunes? Is this imprinted in their bones? Was it second nature for them to be protective of their wealth?

Maybe circumstances brought this reaction to the surface, and in fact, it had nothing to do with the other person at all?

And even when she found herself imagining him in front of her eyes, in the worst light as possible, she was still undoubtedly drawn to him.

Chapter *XXXI*

AND EVEN THOUGH SHE IS SWEET AND OPEN TO HIM, AT THE SAME TIME, SHE IS STARTING TO WEIGH HER OPTIONS AND POSSIBILITIES.

Henry feels her doubts and suspicion; there is no question about it.

He sees that there is always something at the back of Dana's mind.

And he knows what it is.

Of course, the loss of trust he had felt in her makes him angry and puts him in a mood ready to give it all up.

This is what he somehow expected in a way – people around him and their small minds.

Instead of trying to ease Dana's suspicions, Henry started going back to closing himself up again and not communicating.

Back to his good old cabin.

Who was she that he should have to explain himself to her anyhow?!

Their touch was electric. Even in small, delicate doses, it kept sending chills down through their skin.

A stroke behind the elbow, gentle touching of the shoulders next to one another to a bit more serious, his hand on her back (still quite shyly), leading her through the path.

To an occasional kiss.

Never too long, but never interrupted. As he behaved, he had no place to hurry. No place to be. Not so fast. He was just there for her and the slowly building tension made her feel even more.

She dreamed of him touching her in places she wouldn't even dream of.

Chapter XXXII

MAYBE THEY WERE PARTNERS ALL ALONG. Get acquainted with a few rich girls, kidnap and hold one of them, and then get into the favours of the others in the closer family.

To take advantage of them, because they were right now in a vulnerable spot. And Dana's wealth was eventually going to be quite enormous; after all, this situation they were now in was just a small hiccup. In time.

It sounded like almost an impossible plan…but still possible.

In some circles, it would be quite easily known that she and her mother had gotten themselves into this precarious situation.

And maybe just as easy for others to find out that her mother, Sheryl, was in fact inclined to the unexplainable or supernatural phenomena. That there was a respect and fear of these things in her.

Or perhaps Henry was the leading man after all. The old shop owner who abducted Debra Lee just followed in his footsteps, made good on his goals.

All of it was just poppycock, all nonsense…

But maybe he was playing a difficult chess game with her, and the kidnapper was just a pawn…And he killed him in the end.

The police were still unsure; they weren't saying what exactly happened to him. Was he killed in the shootout or in a different way, before? They didn't release any details.

Beautiful, smart and cunning.

Dana remembered that she used to go to the wetlands quite a lot, even in the years before all this, whenever she was visiting here.

Without Debra Lee of course, alone.

An easy mark would she be probably, when you realise that she, and her family's mansion, is sitting right under his nose.

99

Their romance would not be something out of the pink-red bound novels, not at all, she was sure.

Just the opposite, to someone it may sound like a nightmare. Well, why not?

But still there was this natural fear for her own safety.

Not to get unknowingly trapped into somebody else's web, no. She didn't want that at all.

That was not her idea of freedom.

Being taken advantage of.

She was open to living on the edge...but she needed to have all the information!

And all these fantasies she made up could be looked upon as just the result of a tired body and mind...But there was this one thing that stood out.

How was he able to find Debra Lee?

How did he know where she was?

So exactly...so fast.

It was just as probable that he had been the one to put her in that place beforehand!

Just as likely as the fact he would be really psychic.

And the way he so cleverly talked himself out of talking to the police about this, at all...

How smoothly done.

Since Debra Lee was found, they hadn't even held an interview with him since.

She remembered how important this was to him from the very beginning.

At that time to her, it just seemed to be expected. Who wants to talk to the police!

Nothing suspicious.

But now...

Now it was possible to put it all together into this bizarre mosaic.

What if all of his actions were done premeditatedly?

If this was the case, then what she still couldn't understand was how he could foretell their own reactions.

There were so many things – that she and her mother had done – that could not been seen ahead!

So was he...a bit of a psychic, after all?

He knew what would happen, in the end. Seen it beforehand, in his dream, in his cabin, all alone. A girl, disappearing into thin air. And then he decided it was a good plan for him, to get in on this? Grab a little something for himself?

If only just to mess with her, situate himself into her life. Not caring about the missing girl – at all.

Or maybe Henry really saw things in his mind and found Debra Lee on the very first day she went missing. He talked to, and confronted the antique shop owner, who was obviously not very well in the head, and struck a deal with him.

And Henry then continued with a plan of his own, a gamble, that he was somehow able to get into her and her mother's heads. There was no wrong outcome, no definitive goal, he was leading it all to, just to aim, then to play and hoping it all fell into his favour somehow…

How twisted.

Just like a creator. Moving along and playing with all of the pieces involved.

This sounded even more like him, the mastermind behind it all.

And she was his prey, a fool to him (and for him, now!).

Caught in his net, like an exotic butterfly.

Flapping her wings but finding it impossible to get herself out.

This is actually how she feels most of the time with him.

So with all these theories running around in her paranoid head, it was almost impossible to stay in the moment while talking to him, while being with him – to ease into their otherwise sweet bickering and small-talk.

And of course, all this was visible on her face, quite easily. While she was facing him, talking to him, she just couldn't hide that from him.

How would she do that?

Chapter *XXXIII*

THE WIND WAS HOWLING. This was it.

Dana could feel it, in her bones.

The end, the end of everything.

Then when she woke, everything seemed normal.

On contrary to her dream, everything seemed to be just beginning around her.

Yet she could still not shake the unsettled feeling.

She got out of bed with a final resolute, and opened up a window.

A breath of fresh air came from the outside, the smell of sweet pine needles.

But it was still cold. She shivered slightly and stepped away.

She needed something to get back in her old groove. She needed Jonathan, or so she thought.

She hadn't talked to him for days, but it felt like ages. It was since before this all started happening, and when Debra Lee hadn't yet been found.

She would go to see him, but not for him. Just for herself, so that she would feel better.

She didn't know how he was taking it all in, or what he even knew.

They used to be quite close – so who better to help her get in touch with herself again?

How was she supposed to feel after all that happened?

She wanted to feel sweet, unintrusive, naïve and innocent again...as she maybe was when with Jonathan. Or perhaps she never was like that at all, the truth be told, but still she felt the longing to be like that, just a doll to be held.

Little did she know that he didn't see her like that at all. In fact, the way he saw her was exactly the opposite. Interesting how perception is everything, unique to each and every one of us, it is really what tells us apart, makes us who we are.

Or who we want to be.

She didn't want to be just some paranormal vixen for Henry – at least not today.

That is what Henry had made her feel. The irony was that she could be just that, if she wanted it enough.

She hadn't seen Henry for one and a half days. One and a half days. That long.

She couldn't imagine how odd that now was.

Ever since they had started this bizarre friendship, they had never been apart from each other that long.

She was not sure how they left things. She could feel his soft lips on hers, but also his disapproving of her. His disappointment.

They had said some words. Not much.

She could feel it, like hot winds from the desert being replaced by the cool breaths of the mountain, and this sensation just beneath her skin…

Then there was her desire to own him and control him. And just like that…she hated him. She didn't know where and when this got into her, but it was there.

And he was probably a man that was not swayed or manipulated so easily.

So he resented Dana for wanting to do just that, so it began to be a two-way street.

She was outside now, back on the path, she would get in touch with herself again.

And with her wild, unpredictable side as well.

That got her thinking: how easy it would be for her to use Henry for her fun and her advantage, like a paper doll, and then just throw him away!

Her boots comfortably glided over the ground and the damp soil.

If she could just go back to how things were before…but before when?

Debra Lee was back at home, so everything was great, she tried to convince herself.

She smiled lightly. A little bit. Relieved, light-hearted.

She would go and see Henry after. She was sure about it.

But then it hit her, again, a heavy scent. The damp smell of roses.

She looked around and there was…nothing there.

She shuddered slightly.

She knew she must be close to the place where she had seen the flowers, being alone in the wilderness, just a few days ago.

She should have known that they…wouldn't let her go so easily.

It was not easy at all. She was sure it meant something significant, she just wasn't sure what yet. What kind of alluring yet terrifying enchantment was this?

It lay heavily on her chest now. Her intuition. This is the end. It must be. There must be something they still want from her. Something they whisper. Not to her, at least not now. She took a few more steps forward.

Now she saw them.
Dark red all over.
Lost in the wilderness.
Like she was.

Chapter XXXIV

THANKS TO THE ROSES, DANA CAME INTO JONATHAN'S CABIN IN A VERY DIFFERENT MOOD THAN SHE HAD SET OUT FOR IN THE FIRST PLACE. She was a bit flustered, breathing heavily.

"So she is back?!"

Jonathan turned to her with this question.

There was excitement in his eyes. He was beaming.

"This is such great news. I am so happy for you."

He put his hands on Dana's hips and tried to lift her up gently.

Then she realised, she is not happy at all.

And she had to pretend...again. About Debra Lee, again. To be relieved and emotional about it. Just as when she had gone missing.

She lets herself out of his embrace.

Turns her back to him, so he doesn't see she is upset.

She smiles slightly.

"Yes," she says obligingly.

Tears ran in her eyes. She was angry.

"You must all be relieved. Oh, honey. Do you want some tea, coffee?"

He kissed her lightly on the cheek.

"Of course. She is our angel. Everybody is happy," she said in a serious tone.

Jonathan said, "What do you mean? You say it as if you don't mean it."

Dana didn't agree.

"Of course I do. What do you mean?"

They were quiet for a while.

That peaceful feeling, of being at ease, what she was so looking forward to when going to Jonathan's house, had yet to arrive.

She looked anxiously out of the window toward the next-door cabin, as if to see if someone was there.

Jonathan was moving around in the kitchen.

"We should celebrate."

He turned and held her, moving into a kiss.

It was slow, gentle, getting more passionate.

I could get used to this, Dana had thought to herself. *If only it would never end. If he wouldn't stop.*

He stopped, eventually.

And it was all gone. She was feeling cold. It was not enough for her.

She was feeling weak to her knees, panic had stricken her.

What had felt exciting a moment ago, now felt...not so much anymore.

She, a married woman?

It came into her mind so suddenly. Caged indeed, yet free to be her own person.

For him, to him...

Did it make any sense that she could want this?

Nevertheless, she was drawn back to Henry. She could not leave him behind, could she? Why was that?

This relationship with him occupied her mind. Even though, of course, his request had no bearing in the reality. Nothing he could hold her or her mother accountable for.

It just occupied her thoughts. And she was sure his as well.

A sweet haunting.

And he had put that thought there, into her, deliberately. She knew that Henry knew that she was suspicious of him. About this whole operation: the last few days and his help. And that she probably blamed him.

How did he know?

He probably is psychic.

She didn't tell him anything of how she had felt. But she knew that he did know, somehow. Just knew.

But that was not how she really feels about him, in her soul: not really!

Only a part of her brain believed that all these crazy notions might be true.

That he was a conman, or even a criminal, a kidnapper...

The other part of her did not!

So why did Henry pick on only the part of her that did?

The dark was slowly setting in outside. It was probably going to rain soon. Dark clouds. The light had disappeared. She didn't know what to do.

So she kissed Jonathan passionately now, took his face into her hands.

Nothing is better now that Debra Lee is back.

Jonathan was surprised but reciprocated the kiss.

She leaned back – and looked at him, and Jonathan knew that he was probably seeing her for the last time. How did he know…? And then Dana was out of his door, on his porch.

But his breath was taken away, either way.

Chapter *XXXV*

LIKE A BUTTERFLY CAUGHT IN HIS NET.

"You have been to see him?" Henry asked.

He seemed angry, unsettled even.

Dana was out of breath.

It was just a few moments later.

She started with a simple question. "How are you?"

"Good enough, thank you," he replied right back at her.

She sensed he was irritated, and as the dark was settling around the cabin, he closed the curtains on the one side. Probably so that Jonathan wouldn't see.

And that was the last thought Dana would give to Jonathan for a very long time.

Her mind was completely focused now. On something new.

Henry did not turn on the light. She was glad, she didn't need it.

He turned to her.

"This is the first time I am inside here actually."

"Yes. Do you like it?" he said politely. That seemed to calm him down.

"How is she doing?" Henry still couldn't hide the hostility in his voice.

So much between them that was unsaid.

He didn't like her to be suspicious of him, not at all. On the contrary. He hated it.

Dana was willing to forget all about her suspicions of him...if he would just hold her. Now.

He thought to himself:

She is here. Fiery copper hair and bright starlight eyes, in his rooms.

His. Almost.

"She is good, I think."

"And you and your mother?"

"Trying to find our rhythm again, really."

"I know…" he said, but he couldn't finish. "I know that you don't believe me. That I am innocent. That I am, what I say I am. Not some liar. You are the one that is not a believer. How can you do this to me?"

"Don't." She put a finger on his lips.

She was unable to continue. "Just don't," she said in a whisper.

Her lips were red. He kissed her.

Slowly they melted into each other.

For Dana, the feeling was right. It was like where she belonged.

For Henry, he was in a frenzy, a whirlwind of thoughts and emotions in his head.

She slowly moved them towards the bed.

Gradually, his busy mind was able to put his thoughts, concentration, just on to her; her breaths, taking in the same sweet, fresh forest air surrounding them.

He was settled and calm.

He laid her smoothly on his bed.

Gentle layers of clothes, which were revealing her skin – one by one.

For Dana: But right in this moment, it was too much for her. This felt way too predictable to her. More ordinary, more common than what she wanted! She didn't know why she was feeling like she did. Why was that?

For Henry: He still couldn't shake the feeling what if she didn't believe him – entirely – in his version about what happened with her cousin; it hurt him.

This was worthless like that to him – being really close to her, for it to mean something.

Their two bodies to be intertwined, like branches of trees fighting for its way up in the treacherous soils of the wetlands.

Swaying, moving in the wind, but heading into a place where they will be firmly connected.

She felt his unease…Now, instead of it being nice, they started struggling. They put an end to it, halted it. They stopped altogether.

She straightened herself up on the bed.

She wiped her face with the back of her hand, tears mirroring in the corners of her eyes.

It was already dark in the room, he was lost, he hadn't found a way out.

Lost in the situation, he didn't know what to say to her.

Chapter XXXVI

BACK AT HOME, DANA'S MOTHER WAS DISTANT AS IF THERE WERE SUDDENLY THINGS SHE DIDN'T WANT TO SHARE WITH HER.

Sheryl couldn't look her straight in the eyes.

It was as if her mother was suddenly unappreciative of the whole thing that went down with the psychic – and her own daughter being a part in all of it.

Dana was sure: *it will pass. She will have her mother back again soon.*

But she was afraid that her mother was becoming just like one of them – controlling, secretive, conceited and cold. So not like her mother at all. If this wasn't the horrible price she had to pay to be 'let in'? To become an insider, finally after all those years…To be a part of them – their own close family – Mother had to behave like them as well. Or so it would seem to Dana.

Sink into their monotonous ways.

Leaving her, Dana, behind, for some inexplicable reason.

No! Because it was just in her mind.

Nothing else to worry about.

Something else was on her mind as well.

She just had to get used to being without him, now.

Because she hadn't heard from Henry: he had left, gone back to the big city.

He had gone back to where he had belonged anyway, all along.

She couldn't say she was surprised.

But disappointed, it pricked her…that yes.

She learned from others that he had decided to leave…and there was no way of knowing when he would back again. Duty was calling him, he had said.

If he returned, and who knows when, would she even be here?

The reason why it had ended so suddenly she did not grasp.

But she knew it was the beginning of something, bigger them themselves, between them, and not the end. The feeling had got a really tight grip on her.

Again, she had to open the window at night while she was in bed, to let the evening air into her lungs.

The stars on the skies were bright and sure of themselves. On the contrary of her own confused feelings!

How much of her own work, and effort, was needed so this strange destiny of hers was fulfilled?

Or if she did have to just wait?

She was sure that Henry will make good on the promise he had received from her mother, that she would give her to him. In some shape or form. She didn't know how, but it would happen one way or another.

She couldn't shake this feeling; she didn't even know if she wanted to.

All he wanted…was just to take possession of her. Coming from him, it was such a strange thing to ask, to require – the only thing he wanted. She was the most important part in all of this. And that made her feel something.

The unknown pleasures of things that she may never get.

She was thinking this was perpetually hanging over her head, even now, lying in her own safe bed. Her mother hadn't mentioned it even in one simple word. She got nothing from her. As if it was something for her daughter to resolve herself, to her own liking.

And Dana felt that she couldn't really escape from what her mother had told him on that day, talking about her, instead of allowing her to speak for herself. Yet her mother had to decide, Dana was trying to justify her mother's words; she needed to act fast in the moment, like she always did to get things done – finished and accomplished. That is what she had taught her. *Act fast, Dana.* Not to get mixed up in all of her feelings.

She couldn't do that for herself – no, really, wow. She couldn't promise anything to anyone…In that moment, but not in any other, it was not her style. But wasn't now the time that she would be able to?

She felt she couldn't run and hide for cover like she always did.

She was just too curious for that, for what would happen next.

She wondered whether she was supposed to be as cool as the call of the night owl in the dark, or was she supposed to succumb to the heat calling out to her through her veins?

Chapter *XXXVII*

OUTSIDE, THERE WERE SMALL CRYSTALS OF SNOW GLITTERING IN THE AFTERNOON HALF-LIGHT.

Dana was in the city. She was looking for Henry's building or his hotel room; she just had the address. She had to move herself between honking cars, and humbug, something she grew so unused to while living in the marshes for the few weeks.

That was the direction she had decided to take.

He was expecting her.

And yet always being not quite prepared for her.

When she came into his room with all her force and heat, it was just something he wasn't used to. He could never get used to it being just like that, with her.

"So you just leave, go away?" she smiled, but she was not happy.

"Abandon me, with them!?" Her eyes were wild and there was a spark of provocation in them as she continued.

Henry suddenly realised that he was not the only one with the need to run away from something – the people in his life. She had that feeling too, that urge.

"What are you talking about exactly, Dana?" he tried insinuating that he doesn't know what this was about. "What is it that you really want from me?" he went on to tease.

She walked around the apartment, looked out of the window. Only now she started to notice things in the room surrounding her. It was all decorated in darker tones, stylish, but nothing much stood out. It came to her it may be just a paid-for room, or it was actually the place he lived in, his own apartment.

Dana knew so little about him she couldn't even recognise whether the objects around her were his possessions, in his own style and taste, or not.

The state of the place didn't really matter because she just had known she had to come here.

Looking out the window at the view from this highest floor, the world felt different; beyond the city, shining through were the wetlands, her present home at the moment.

The sounds were different, the lights unnatural...and then there was him.

It awakened something in her, something she knew she wasn't letting go.

Not yet. Couldn't let it slip through her fingers – that was not like her.

Turning from the window, her face almost in the dark, she put on a serious tone.

The whole room was now between them.

This is a way for her to go.

Just for her. Without the prejudices of her family and their will, without their deciding about her future, taking over control of her life. As they had planned all along, that she would just get in line and obey them. As it had been with her father, and her mother, anyway up until now.

She did not know what she was headed for, certainly, but just now she just didn't care anymore. She was ready.

"You know we had an agreement. The one you made with my mother. The one, if you help us...to succeed in what we wanted... you will want me, to keep me."

As your reward. If that is even possible, to have and 'to keep' another person.

To really control them, even to know them at all. And if you don't know a person, don't know his soul...but how ever can you, is it even possible?

Looking at him, it was somewhat obvious; he was so handsome right now, but he didn't want that anymore. He didn't want her. She wondered why.

"How long I am supposed to wait about with what you decide to do about it...to have this thing hanging over my head?" she said pleadingly, yet wistfully.

To have this uncertainty. He didn't want her. She couldn't breathe. *That could not be true*, she told herself.

Henry started speaking, almost to himself.

"You don't believe me. I know you don't. And what is the worst…you have stopped trusting me. You don't trust me."

He stopped. As if it was all. This was his reaction to all she had said. This was the problem.

Nothing to add.

Now here it was. She knew that he knew. All her suspicions. Crazy fantasies, maybe. It was coming. That he in fact orchestrated the whole thing with Debra Lee, to get in their good graces; he was no psychic, not at all. Dana believed that.

"It doesn't matter," she said, in her defence. "It is not the truth."

She couldn't continue.

"Just talk to me." It all didn't ring true when said out loud. "Just talk to me."

"This not how I imagined it," he finished for her.

Henry was having these thoughts, thinking them without telling her.

She is different! It will be different. But she does not believe and accept that part of him that makes him different from all the others. And this is what he cares about now.

That he could be open with her – and not like he was with everybody else!

She did not accept him, as he hoped she would. That was not lost on him.

This is not what he wanted. This is not what he needed.

Then, he decided to tell her *just* that.

He ended it with, "This like that, has no worth or value for me, whatsoever."

He turned his back to Dana, almost facing the wall close behind him. The liquor glasses and bottles on the small stylish bar table beside him rattled with his movement.

She leaned towards him, and he turned gravely away. She placed her lean arms on his shoulders. Her eyes alive, face pale.

He continued to think. How could he just take one look at her and then unravel completely? The one thing he was always hiding from, the one thing he couldn't do…anytime, anywhere: to show and explore his true self, with no shame. Seeing her made him want to. Like there was no other way.

She was staring back into his eyes…He wanted to relax, to stop controlling himself in any way. Let himself be carried away, not be alert all the time.

Her excitement and frustration were intoxicating.

She exclaimed in frustration,

"Why can't things be like they were before?"

Before Debra Lee was found.

Between them. Things were…Debra Lee was dead. She was supposed to be, stay dead.

They had this rapport between them, they had a place for one another. For this relationship. No doubts, the trust was there naturally.

"Why can't we have that? That is what was meant to be for us. If only we could go back. Everything is not lost yet. Don't you give up on me. There is a solution, for both of us."

Then in the moment, an idea came.

A reflection in the darkness.

And it brought something new with it.

THIS IS what was supposed to happen. This was how it was meant to be.

He smiled at her.

"Okay," he answered even before she said what came to her right now, out loud:

"Let's kill her."

Something important had happened to them when they met.

When we met, Debra Lee…was dead. Or at least, she was missing. Wasn't she? Did that really happen?

They were connected by something special, out of the ordinary, that made everything just glimmer, be extraordinary; their partnership made sense…by a purpose. Only to have it all taken away from them; it was not fair!

They would do anything to just bring it back to being as it was…instead of having it all just taken away from them, with no sense of purpose at all.

Just left with doubts, about themselves, about everything.

She was living on the edge, and she was more open, open to him…because of it.

He was looking for this all along…for her.

His whole life, so to say.

Epilogue

THEY HELD HER UNDER THE WATER.

Her long hair getting wet… and soaked, heavy body under their arms.

It was dark.

A pitch-black night, out on the wetlands.

No animals or owls tonight, it was quiet.

It took as long as was necessary. She didn't resist, almost not at all.

Nor make any sound.

It was not simple for them…*She has just…*This is what everyone thought had happened to her. Here, out in the woods.

So tonight, she has met her fate. Just a little bit later.

This is what was supposed to happen to Debra Lee.

Everything around was calm, just as it should be.

They turned back the time.

Changed things.

Brought them back to the way it was.

Just a sweet scent was coming to them, on the soft wind, as if reminiscing.

Roses, flowers, but already decaying in the heavy night air.

THE END

About the Author

BARBARA COOPER BELIEVES THERE IS MORE TO LIFE — AND TO LOVE —THAN MEETS THE EYE. A lifelong fan of beautiful writing, she educated herself in law at university, earning a doctorate degree, and making a name with her works on legal history. Yet she could not escape the siren song of her imagination. When *Harrowing Roses* came to her in a dream, she picked up her pen and got to work. Barbara lives in a lake-house surrounded by a landscape imbued with history and magic. She often walks along the nearby water, accompanied by her cats, when they are in the mood.

She enjoys contemplating the unknown through the medium of stories, being a big fan of magic, poetry and the paranormal.

Acknowledgments

TO MY CHARACTERS, FOR BEING WHO THEY ARE AND BRINGING THIS STORY TO LIFE.

To my *dream*, which transported me to a place at once terrifying and yet inviting, a world of vast bodies of water, lonely woods, so different from anything I had known before...*and dark, velvety flowers.*

And to every being who helped me along the way: *thank you.*

Notes

Notes

Notes

Notes

Lightning Source UK Ltd.
Milton Keynes UK
UKHW022032210922
409227UK00007B/99